"What do you want, Doctor?" Captain Janeway replied over the comm. "We're rather busy up here."

"Kes has told me we're in a battle . . ." the doctor-program said, "one that might last for thirty years."

"That's right, Doctor," the captain snapped back, "the battle might last for thirty years, but *we* won't if we don't get out of here. Bridge out."

The doctor turned to Kes. "The captain was serious?"

Kes nodded.

"We might be destroyed?"

"It's possible," Kes said calmly, "but I certainly hope we won't be."

Look for STAR TREK Fiction from Pocket Books

Star Trek: The Original Series

Star Trek: The Next Generation

Star Trek: Deep Space Nine

Star Trek: Voyager

STAR TREK VOYAGER™

RAGNAROK

NATHAN ARCHER

POCKET BOOKS

New York   London   Toronto   Sydney   Tokyo   Singapore

An *Original* Publication of POCKET BOOKS

POCKET BOOKS, a division of Simon & Schuster Inc.
1230 Avenue of the Americas, New York, NY 10020

This book is published by Pocket Books, a division of
Simon & Schuster Inc., under exclusive license from
Paramount Pictures.

ISBN: 0-671-52044-X

First Pocket Books printing July 1995

10 9 8 7 6 5 4 3 2 1

POCKET and colophon are registered trademarks of
Simon & Schuster Inc.

Printed in the U.S.A.

Dedicated to
Ephraim E. diKahble
&
David Joseph Oznot

CHAPTER
1

FOR THE MOMENT, ALL WAS WELL ABOARD THE FEDERAtion starship *Voyager*.

While there were repairs being made, and they were, as always, short-handed, there were no life-threatening emergencies at the moment. The engines were working well, life support was functioning, the hydroponics plant in the forward cargo bay was flourishing; they were well clear of any inhabited systems or hostile craft.

This relatively relaxed situation meant that Captain Kathryn Janeway could afford to take the time to think ahead, to plan out exactly where the ship was headed, and that was just what she was doing as she and Neelix stood on the central level of the ship's bridge, studying their charts.

Around them, the rest of the *Voyager*'s command crew went about their business, black-shod feet silent on the soft gray carpeting, hands moving quickly across the gleaming black panels, eyes watching the illuminated blue and gold displays. The low humming of the ship's engines was a constant, reassuring background sound, punctuated every so often by the hiss of an automatic door opening. Janeway and Neelix paid no attention to any of that; they were focused on the navigation screens. Neelix leaned forward, both hands on the smooth black console, while Janeway stood nearby, holding on to the chrome rail that ran between the upper and central levels of the bridge. Both of them were considering what course they should take.

Obviously, their general direction was back toward the Alpha Quadrant and the Federation—she had promised the crew she would get them home, no matter how long it took, and Captain Janeway intended to keep that promise.

Still, they couldn't simply head off in a straight line across the galaxy. There would have to be more stops along the way; they would need to replenish certain supplies, find ways to repair damaged equipment. The ship's replicators were no longer entirely functional, and were never able to provide everything they needed, in any case—replicator technology had its limits. Some things couldn't be reliably replicated—including some of the essential elements that powered the replicators.

So there would be stops for supplies. There would probably have to be stops simply to give the crew a chance to breathe fresh air and move about unconfined by steel bulkheads, as well—that was essential for morale. Visits to the holodeck only went so far toward delaying the inevitable cabin fever; one hundred and forty people who knew they were probably going to be confined to the same ship for years on end *needed* chances to get out on a planetary surface, to look at open skies and breathe unfiltered air every so often.

At least the holodeck's energy systems were incompatible with the rest of the ship, so that there was no reason to shut it down to conserve their precious resources—the energy it consumed couldn't have been used elsewhere in any case. Keeping it activated was an emotional necessity. The crew needed somewhere to unwind.

But it wasn't enough.

Stops would have to be made.

And the question was therefore *where* these stops should be made.

While Starfleet had, of course, programmed complete star maps of the entire galaxy into the ship's computers, those were limited, providing little more than the location and spectral type of each star. That had been enough information to tell them almost instantly where they were when they had been snatched across the galaxy, but it wasn't much help in planning their route home.

Smaller or less stable and obvious bodies—such as planets, anomalies, dust clouds, or magnetic storms—were not included in the star maps. The *Voyager* carried no charts, no records, no descriptions of any of the worlds or civilizations it might encounter in this part of the galaxy, nor of any dangerous phenomena, such as plasma storms, ahead.

The ship's computers could provide vast quantities of information about virtually every inhabited body or energy field in the Alpha Quadrant, as well as a good-sized slice of the Beta Quadrant and even those relatively tiny areas near the Gamma Quadrant wormhole that had been charted—but the *Voyager* was in the Delta Quadrant, yanked across to the far side of the galaxy by an extragalactic alien being known as the Caretaker, and then left to its own devices.

The Federation knew nothing about the local hazards of the Delta Quadrant. No Federation vessel had ever come here before the *Voyager*'s unplanned arrival.

So, as explorers of every kind had done before her, Kathryn Janeway had taken on a native guide, a local inhabitant who claimed to be completely familiar with most of the various planets and their inhabitants in the vicinity.

He doubled as a cook and handyman, but the Talaxian who called himself Neelix had been taken aboard the *Voyager* primarily as a guide.

And today Captain Janeway had summoned that guide to the bridge, where he stood a meter away from her, bent over a navigation panel.

He didn't have to bend very far; Neelix was shorter than the average human, though he made up for some of that with an exhuberant personality.

His clothing was brightly polychrome, garish in comparison with the subdued grays and blues and silver of the *Voyager*'s interior. Janeway supposed that among his fellow Talaxians Neelix might well be considered tall and handsome, and his attire the height of fashion, as he sometimes claimed, but by human standards he was . . . well, *ugly* was too strong a word.

Comical wasn't too strong. *Comical* fit the bill nicely. She hoped she hadn't let Neelix know that; he had as much pride and self-respect as the next sentient being, and she doubted he'd appreciate knowing that his appearance reminded her of a clown's.

She thought he might suspect it, but that wasn't the same as knowing.

Neelix was basically humanoid. His oddly shaped head was adorned with brownish mottling, sparse tufts of hair, concavities at the temples, pointed and multilayered ears, and a blobby nose that appeared to have been slit down the middle; when that was combined with his taste in clothing the result was definitely clownish.

Still, Neelix was no fool. Janeway watched with interest as he frowned at the diagram on the display screen, one finger tracing along the curving diagram.

"Your star charts are still difficult for me, Captain," he said, "but if I understand this correctly, I think you really ought to change course."

Rather than crowd her guide, Janeway reached over and tapped a control, transferring the star chart and its accompanying readouts from the console to the main viewscreen that stretched across the front of the ship's bridge. She studied it for a moment, then turned to face her alien helper.

"Why?" she asked. "Our sensors don't show anything particularly hazardous on our present course."

"Well, of course," Neelix said with a deferential shrug, "I suppose that would all depend on just what you consider *hazardous.*"

Janeway smiled. "Magnetic storms, supernovae—I'd say that sort of thing qualifies as hazardous. Is there anything like that ahead of us?"

"Well, no," the Talaxian said, drawing out the final syllable thoughtfully. "Nothing like *that,* exactly. But everyone around here generally considers it a good idea to avoid that star cluster ahead." He rounded the end of the forward console, took a few steps toward the large screen, then pointed at the particular group he meant.

"Why?" Janeway demanded again.

"Because of the war, of course. . . ." He saw her expression, and caught himself. "Oh," he said. "Well, I guess you don't know about that."

"No," Janeway said. "What war? Are the Kazon-Ogla active around here?"

The *Voyager*'s crew had already had one run-in with the local group known as the Kazon-Ogla, and Janeway had to admit she wasn't eager for another.

Neelix sighed, and pointed again. "No, not the Kazon-Ogla," he said. "That's the Kuriyar Cluster ahead, where the Hachai and the P'nir live. Unpleasant people." He shook his head in distaste. "They've been at war with each other for as long as anyone can remember—centuries, certainly, and probably for millennia. Even in our very oldest legends, from the first days that Talaxians began to travel in space, the Hachai and P'nir were fighting each other."

"And they're still fighting?" Janeway asked. She stepped away from the rail for a closer look at the screen.

"So far as I know," Neelix said. "I haven't actually gone into the Kuriyar Cluster and *asked* lately, you understand."

"Has anyone else?"

Neelix shook his head. "People around this part of the galaxy have always tried to avoid the Hachai and the P'nir anyway, and walking into the middle of their war is extremely unpopular. They're not always very careful about who they shoot at."

"I see," Janeway said noncommittally.

"Perhaps I've misread your proposed course," Neelix said apologetically, "but it appeared to take us directly through the Kuriyar Cluster."

"It does," Janeway admitted. "You would advise against that?"

"Oh, very much so, Captain." Neelix nodded enthusiastically.

Janeway glanced over toward the turbolift, where Neelix's Ocampa companion Kes was standing and trying hard to be unobtrusive.

Kes's appearance was much closer to human than Neelix's; except for her ears she could have easily passed for a native back on Earth. She looked frail and ethereally beautiful—and, Janeway knew, she was even younger than she appeared, and quite possibly less human than Neelix, despite her outward form. The average Ocampa life span was only nine standard years; Kes, little more than a year old, was a mature adult. She also had hints of some little-understood Ocampa psychic gifts—telepathic projection, and other, less easily defined abilities.

Kes, seeing Janeway's look, nodded vigorously. "I agree," she said.

Janeway wasn't sure whether this agreement meant that Kes actually knew anything about this war, or simply that she was supporting her friend, but it didn't really matter. They had taken Neelix aboard the *Voyager* to act as their native guide, and there was no point in having a native guide if one didn't take his advice.

Janeway was turning to face the main viewscreen again, about to give the order to change course, to take them safely around the star cluster in question, when Harry Kim, the ensign manning the Operations station, suddenly announced, "Captain, we're being scanned—I think. . . ."

He turned, and shouted, "Captain, it's a tetryon beam, a coherent tetryon beam!"

Janeway whirled. "Red alert!" she shouted, grabbing for the railing. "Be ready to brace for impact!"

CHAPTER
2

THE LIGHTS DIMMED INSTANTLY AT THE CAPTAIN'S CALL
for red alert, to permit the bridge crew to focus
more closely on their control panels. Janeway,
gripping the railing, turned to face the Operations
station. That station was a bay set into the port side
of the bridge's upper level, a bay where Ensign
Harry Kim stood, almost surrounded by displays
and controls.

"Ensign, do you read a displacement wave anywhere?" she demanded.

"Negative, Captain," Kim replied, as he quickly
scanned several panels. "No sign of any other
unusual phenomena."

Janeway relaxed slightly, relieved—but also
somewhat disappointed.

Once before, the *U.S.S. Voyager* had been scanned by a coherent tetryon beam—and immediately afterward the ship had been caught in a magnetic displacement wave that had dragged it halfway across the galaxy in an instant. The tetryon beam had been used by the Caretaker to see whether anyone aboard the *Voyager* might suit its purposes, and when it had discovered that there were possibilities—though they hadn't worked out in the end—it had sent the displacement wave to fetch the *Voyager* to its own vicinity.

That journey had been brief and violent, and had left the ship damaged and several of her crew dead or injured; the vacancies had been made up with the crew of a rebel ship, a Maquis ship, that the *Voyager* had been hunting, and that had been similarly abducted.

It had been a rough ride, and furthermore, the abduction had left the *Voyager* stranded tens of thousands of light-years from home.

When another tetryon beam was detected, Janeway's first thought had been that they were about to be hurled back home. When that didn't happen she was relieved to be spared whatever damage the transition might have inflicted, but disappointed that they were not being sent back to the Alpha Quadrant and the Federation.

"Lock our own sensors on to the beam . . ." she began.

"I'm sorry, Captain," Ensign Kim interrupted without turning from the sensor console, "but it's gone. Duration was less than point four seconds."

"Any sign of a recurrence?" Janeway asked. "A cycle, perhaps?"

"No, Captain," Kim answered. "It seems to have been an isolated event."

Janeway frowned. "Cancel red alert," she said; the bridge's normal lighting returned, banishing shadows and restoring the usual soothing colors. The captain stared at the viewscreen for a moment, then turned again to the Ops station.

Harry Kim watched her from behind his controls, ready and eager, anxiously awaiting her orders.

Kim had come aboard the *Voyager* fresh from Starfleet Academy, thoroughly educated and completely trained, but still inexperienced, still a bit naive. His rather round Asian face was open and easily read; he hadn't yet learned to mask anything. He knew his job, understood his duties, but hadn't yet learned to anticipate his captain's wishes, to do, without being told, that little bit extra that would make him a really first-rate operations and communications officer.

It was an amazingly bad bit of luck for him to have had his first mission wind up like this, Janeway thought; his parents, back on Earth, must still be in shock at the disappearance of their pride and joy.

"Ensign Kim," Janeway said, "I want you to review the ship's sensor records. Find out everything you can about that beam—its waveforms and energy signature, where it came from, what it did to us, if anything—whatever the computers can tell us. I want to know just how closely it matches the tetryon beam that the Caretaker used to scan us."

"Yes, Captain," Kim replied, immediately setting to work at his console.

"You think that that beam was the Caretaker's companion checking us out?" Tom Paris asked from his place at the forward control panel, a long, curving console that separated the central and lower levels of the bridge.

The question wasn't one that the officer at the helm should have been asking, really—but then, Tom Paris wasn't really the officer who should have been at the helm. Lieutenant Stadi, the *Voyager*'s regular pilot-navigator, had been killed during the abrupt journey from the Alpha Quadrant, and Paris, a onetime renegade who had been aboard as an observer, had been appointed to fill in.

Paris was an admiral's son, and no one had ever let him forget it—including himself. Janeway was sure that that desperate need to live up to his family's standards had been what led Paris to falsify reports—and then, later, to admit that he had done so, an admission that had gotten him kicked out of Starfleet.

He had probably felt he had nothing left to lose when he joined the Maquis as a mercenary. Janeway supposed, however, that getting caught and landing in a New Zealand prison might have convinced him otherwise.

Maybe Tom Paris was the sort who had to hit bottom before he could start back up; if so, Janeway thought he'd done it, there in that prison camp. It hadn't been a particularly harsh environment in a physical sense, but for an admiral's son who had always thought himself destined for command, it must have been hell knowing where he had been sent, and that by his family's standards he deserved to be there.

But he was on the way back, Janeway was sure. Ever since the Caretaker had grabbed the *Voyager,* Paris had done his best for Janeway and for the ship.

Janeway thought his manners still left something to be desired, though. His question, while reasonable, had the ring of impertinence.

And it was a good question—had that tetryon beam originated with the Caretaker's lost companion?

The being that had snatched *Voyager* from the far side of the galaxy had been called the Caretaker because it had dedicated itself to protecting and caring for a race known as the Ocampa—Kes's race. It had built an immense construction Janeway had, for the lack of a better name, called the Array, and had used that construction to perform whatever tasks it chose to undertake, such as supplying the Ocampa civilization with energy— or scanning and then capturing the *Voyager.*

The Caretaker was dead now, dead and gone, and the Array had been destroyed to keep it out of the hands of those unpleasant locals called the Kazon-Ogla. That left the Ocampa—and the *Voyager*—to their own devices.

Before the Caretaker had died, however, it had

told the crew of the *Voyager* that it had once had a companion, an extragalactic creature like itself, but that this companion had deserted the Caretaker and the Ocampa long ago, centuries ago, to wander the stars.

It seemed a safe assumption that this companion would use the same technology that the Caretaker had used—and Janeway knew of no other source, anywhere in the galaxy, of coherent tetryon beams.

Of course, she didn't know that there weren't other sources, either. No one in the Alpha Quadrant had ever developed tetryonic technology, but the *Voyager* was not *in* the Alpha Quadrant. They had already encountered some technology in the Delta Quadrant unlike anything Janeway had ever seen before.

"I think, Mr. Paris, that it *might* have been the Caretaker's companion," Janeway replied evenly. "I hope to have some actual evidence one way or the other when Ensign Kim completes his study."

"And in the meantime, Captain," Neelix said anxiously, "if I might point out that we are still heading directly into a war zone at incredible speed . . ."

Janeway glanced at the display on the main viewscreen. The *Voyager* was, indeed, headed directly toward the Kuriyar Cluster and traveling there at warp six, but even so, they would not reach it for hours—plenty of time for Harry Kim to review whatever the ship's automatic systems had recorded about the tetryon scan.

"I'm aware of that," she said. "Thank you, Mr.

Neelix." She turned toward the communications station. "Anything, Ensign?"

"Not much, Captain," Kim reported. He leaned forward, looking over his control panel at the captain. "I haven't been able to distinguish any identifying characteristics in the beam—there are no resonance frequencies, no interference patterns, no detectible scatter. It's just pure monoparticulate tetryon radiation. That's the same thing we found when we analyzed the computer records of the Caretaker's scanning beam, but it doesn't really tell us much; I'd think that anyone who could project a beam like that in the first place would be able to keep it this clean."

"Have you located the source?"

Kim shook his head. "I can give you a direction, Captain," he said, "but no range; the beam didn't last long enough for us to triangulate, and without any scatter or Doppler effects . . . well, it could have come from that cluster just ahead of us, or from somewhere back in Alpha Quadrant, or from anywhere in between, for all we can tell."

"What's the direction, then?"

"I'll put it on the screen."

A moment later Kim's diagram appeared on the main viewer; Janeway took one look and smiled wryly.

"It would seem, Mr. Neelix," she said, "that our mysterious scanner lies in exactly the direction that you'd advise us to avoid."

Sure enough, if the *Voyager* were to attempt to backtrack the tetryon beam, it would travel directly through the exact center of the Kuriyar Cluster—assuming that they didn't come across the beam's source before they got that far.

Janeway looked around the bridge at her command crew.

Her first officer, Chakotay, was seated in the right-hand chair of the two set below the rail that divided the upper level of the bridge from the central. He sat there, impassive, calmly awaiting her decision; she knew that he would not hesitate to argue if he thought she was making a disastrously wrong choice, but that he trusted her to do the right thing. He had been the commander of the Maquis ship that the Caretaker had abducted and that the *Voyager* had been hunting, but he had seen the necessity of joining forces, and in the end had sacrificed his own ship to make sure the awesome technology of the Array did not fall into the wrong hands.

Now he served aboard the *Voyager,* replacing her own dead first officer, and he served very well, accepting her authority as captain, but never being slavishly obedient. If he had some strong objection to her plans, he would say so.

Tuvok, the *Voyager*'s Security/Tactical officer, was in his station at the starboard end of the upper level, a bay that mirrored the Operations bay. He was as calm as Chakotay—but he was a Vulcan; he was *always* calm. His serenity was a racial characteristic, where Chakotay's was a sign of his trust in her competence.

Tuvok had been with her for a long time. He, too, knew when to speak up.

Paris, at the helm, was studying his controls, only glancing quickly at Janeway now and then; she thought he was trying to hide his eagerness to venture into danger. Janeway knew the threat of alien warships didn't worry Paris; if anything, he was looking forward to testing his piloting skills—and his courage—against them. Tom Paris, the admiral's son, clearly still felt he had something to prove—to himself, if not necessarily to anyone else.

Harry Kim, on the port side in Operations, was visibly nervous, and was trying hard not to be, or at least not to show it. He wanted to be as fearless as anyone—that was part of his vision of the ideal Starfleet officer, an ideal he desperately wanted to live up to—but he had enough imagination and common sense that he couldn't help thinking just how nasty the situation might get if the *Voyager* ventured into that cluster.

Neelix, down near the viewscreen, was nervous and clearly didn't care who knew it; Janeway guessed that he thought venturing into a known war zone was insane, but he'd seen enough of human behavior—of *her* behavior, specifically—that he knew she was considering it anyway.

And Kes, up by the gray door of the turbolift, was watching them all, fascinated. She probably hadn't given the possibility of death and destruction ahead of them any real thought; she was too interested in observing the people around her to worry about herself.

All but Kes undoubtedly had their own opinions as to whether the *Voyager* should follow that tetryon beam into danger, or avoid the Kuriyar Cluster, but none of them were arguing with Janeway about it; they knew the decision was hers. . . .

"Surely, Captain, you aren't going to risk all our lives, and your lovely ship, just to see where a scanning beam came from?" Neelix asked.

"I'm afraid I am," Janeway replied, reaching the decision everyone had known she would reach. "Mr. Paris, take our heading from Ensign Kim's analysis of the tetryon beam; we will attempt to follow it to its source."

"Aye-aye, Captain," Paris answered promptly, his tone almost gleeful.

"But Captain . . . !" Neelix began.

Janeway looked him silently in the eye, and the little alien stammered, then fell silent.

She almost felt sorry for him. It was true that there was no point in taking on a native guide if you ignored *all* his advice, but Neelix didn't truly appreciate the situation here. If the *Voyager* didn't find a shortcut of some kind, most of her crew—perhaps *all* of her crew—would be dead of old age before the ship reached Federation space.

That assumed that they didn't crack under the strain and kill each other first. And that the *Voyager* could survive that long without proper maintenance.

It was worth taking a few risks—even a few large ones—to avoid any such fate.

Neelix merely wanted to survive, and to enjoy his life, and he was perfectly content aboard the *Voyager,* with a comfortable berth and plentiful food and water and Kes at his side; he wasn't interested in going anywhere in particular.

Janeway could hardly fault him for that, but for her own part, she wanted more, much more. She wanted to return home, to see her lover Mark again, to see her crew safely back to their families.

It was worth taking a few risks for all that—but not foolish ones. She looked to starboard.

"Mr. Tuvok," she said, "I want long-range scanners operating at full military readiness, with shields and phasers on standby. If we're entering a war zone, I want to be ready for anything. It's not our fight, but the locals may not realize that."

"Aye-aye, Captain."

"Very good. Mr. Paris, give us warp seven."

The decision made, Janeway sat back in her chair and watched as the image of the Kuriyar Cluster expanded to fill the screen before her.

CHAPTER
3

JANEWAY SUPPRESSED AN EXASPERATED SIGH AS HER Talaxian guide popped up at her side again the very instant she set foot back on the bridge.

"Captain, *please* reconsider!" Neelix said. "The Hachai and the P'nir have been at war with one another for *centuries;* they've exhausted entire planets building their war fleets. Their ships could be *anywhere.*"

Janeway, who had listened to Neelix's protests for half an hour before retreating to her ready room for five minutes for a respite, paused on the steps and turned to face him at that.

"They could be anywhere? Do you mean they have cloaking technology?" she asked, with interest.

"Have what?" Neelix replied, startled.

"Cloaking technology."

"Ah . . . I don't know what that is," Neelix said. "Perhaps the translator is malfunctioning; I might know it by another name."

"I don't think so, Mr. Neelix," Janeway replied, turning her attention back to the main viewer and proceeding to her chair. "I think it's unknown around this part of the galaxy. Which is just as well."

"Unknown to *me,* perhaps," Neelix said, seeing a possible opportunity, "but does that mean it's unknown to the Hachai? Or the P'nir?"

"Probably," Janeway said dryly.

Neelix, seeing that that particular gambit wasn't going to work, that Janeway was not sufficiently afraid of "cloaking technology" to turn aside merely because the combatants might have it, returned to his basic theme. "Even so," he said, "the Hachai and the P'nir both have fearsome weapons, and they have *thousands* of warships cruising the cluster, shooting at everything they see."

"Everything?" Janeway asked, as she looked over at Neelix again.

"Yes, Captain, everything!" Neelix said enthusiastically. "You see, throughout the war, the P'nir have used many ruses in their attempts to gain the advantage—they've had warships disguised as neutral trading vessels, bombs disguised as asteroids or wreckage, and so on. You can imagine the havoc they produced!"

"Yes," Janeway acknowledged. "I can see that." She studied the viewscreen; they were approaching a star on the outskirts of the Kuriyar Cluster, a young main-sequence star that could reasonably be expected to have planets.

If one of those planets was M-class the *Voyager* might be able to pick up a few supplies, and the crew might take a brief shore leave.

"Well," Neelix continued, "as a result of those tricks, the Hachai became understandably distrustful of *anything* unfamiliar that passed through their space. The last several ships that came into the cluster and attempted to trade with the Hachai were given one warning, then fired upon—the Hachai took them to be more P'nir trickery."

"Interesting," Janeway said. "And the P'nir? Are they equally afraid of Hachai deception?"

Neelix shook his head. "No, no. The P'nir are . . . well, the P'nir are the P'nir. They live by a strict code of their own, a code that doesn't acknowledge the value of anything that's not part of the P'nir hierarchy. They don't recognize any authority or any rights but their own. I'd say that if the Hachai weren't fighting them, somebody else would be—they don't make friends easily."

Janeway's mouth quirked in a half-smile.

"Indeed," she said, leaning on one elbow.

"Really," Neelix said. "The P'nir have never been any good at trade; they prefer piracy. Not that *they* call it that, of course. If they admitted it was piracy, that would mean acknowledging that other species could own something in the first place, and the P'nir just don't think that way." He shrugged. "At any rate, the P'nir gave up all trade or other contact with other races long ago, because it distracted them from the war effort against the Hachai."

"They do sound quite unpleasant, Mr. Neelix," Janeway agreed.

"Oh, they *are!*" Neelix said. "Captain, if the Hachai spot you, they'll probably give you one warning before they open fire, but if the P'nir see you and decide to notice you at all, they won't even do that—they'll fire or not at the whim of whatever captain you meet. Please, you *really* don't want to take your beautiful, *comfortable* ship into the Kuriyar Cluster."

Neelix looked around the bridge for support, but quickly saw that he wasn't going to get it. Tom Paris, at the forward console, was ignoring the entire conversation and keeping his attention on the helm; on either side of the bridge Harry Kim and Tuvok were listening and seemed interested, but neither of them showed any sign of siding with Neelix, a mere passenger, against their captain.

The first officer might have been willing to argue with the captain, but Neelix couldn't tell whether Commander Chakotay had heard a word of what he'd said. That man was a puzzle to Neelix; he couldn't make out Chakotay's thinking. Right now, Chakotay was sitting in his place on the bridge, relaxed, watching the viewscreen, and Neelix could not read the man's expression at all. Was he calm? Bored? Angry? Was he studying the screen, or simply watching those little indicator lights above and below the screen?

Neelix couldn't tell. He couldn't tell whether Chakotay was listening, or ignoring the entire discussion in favor of his own thoughts.

As for Janeway herself, she was listening, as she had been all along, but her mind was made up. She had faith in her ship and her crew, and thought they were ready to face any ordinary dangers, and the possible benefits offered by the Kuriyar Cluster—or rather, by the tetryon beam that might have come from the cluster—were too great to be ignored.

Furthermore, in addition to the possibilities that tetryon beam presented, there was also the question of her duties as a Starfleet officer. The Federation was dedicated to peace. Oh, the Prime Directive did not allow them to intervene directly, but Starfleet had always devoted great effort to peacemaking; the Federation provided negotiators, ferried diplomats, served as arbitrator, and otherwise did whatever it could to end interstellar war.

As a Starfleet officer, Janeway felt it was her duty, if she encountered these warring nations Neelix described, to see if she could help make peace. Under the circumstances that the *Voyager* found itself in she was not going to go around looking for trouble, and she could have lived with her conscience if they had simply dodged the Kuriyar

Cluster in the first place, but adding the mysterious scan on top of that . . .

Well, she intended to go through that cluster, war or no war, regardless of what Neelix might say.

She wished Neelix would just accept the situation and stop arguing. She was tempted to throw him off the bridge—but if he really *did* know something about what lay ahead, if there really *were* hostile warships out there ready to pounce, the Talaxian's knowledge might be vital, and they might well need it instantly.

"Mr. Paris," she said, "scan that system ahead of us, and see if there's anything we could use."

"Aye-aye, Captain," Paris replied. "I understand the replicators have been malfunctioning again; I'll just see if I can find a coffee plantation, shall I?"

"That would be fine, Mr. Paris," Janeway replied, smiling at the joke. "Or perhaps a sign telling us where to find the Caretaker's companion."

"Captain, please," Neelix said, coming to stand beside her, one hand on the railing. "What would the Caretaker's companion be doing in the middle of a war?"

"Perhaps trying to *end* the war," Janeway replied, her smile vanishing as she tried not to sound as exasperated with Neelix as she was beginning to feel. "After all, we know from the Caretaker's behavior in regard to the Ocampa that these extra-galactic creatures do seem to be benign in their intentions, if not always in their actions. Perhaps attempts to stop the war have kept her busy—that might be why you've heard nothing about the companion's presence elsewhere, Mr. Neelix."

"But if she were as powerful as the Caretaker, and she wanted to end the war, she *would* have," Neelix protested. "The P'nir and the Hachai don't have anything close to *that* sort of technology!"

"But we don't know how she might think," Janeway said. "She might be limited in her actions—as we are limited by the Prime Directive, Mr. Neelix. The Caretaker seems to have been bound by a powerful moral code, and perhaps that code won't allow the companion to intervene directly. But she might be there, trying to talk sense to the Hachai and the P'nir."

"Well, if she is, it isn't working," Neelix said dourly—or at least, as dourly as the little Talaxian could manage. "They were still fighting the last *I* heard, and whether she's there or not I expect them to keep fighting for years."

"Well, whether she's there or not," Janeway said, "if we run into the Hachai or the P'nir, perhaps *we* can talk some sense into them."

"Ha!" Neelix burst out. "You think you can stop a war that's lasted *centuries?*"

"It might be," Tuvok suggested from behind and above the Talaxian, "that after so long a conflict, the Hachai and the P'nir are ready to see how illogical their war is. Perhaps we can act as the catalyst necessary to end it."

"I think you underestimate how stubborn they are," Neelix said without turning.

"And I think *you* underestimate how stubborn

we are," Janeway retorted. "Not to mention what we're capable of handling. Our home lies in this direction, and that tetryon beam, which may well indicate a shorter route home, *also* came from this direction. We're willing to take a few risks—"

"Captain," Paris interrupted suddenly, "I think you should see this."

Startled, Janeway turned away from Neelix to see Paris sitting at the pilot's console, staring at a display. She rose, stepped forward, and looked down over Paris's shoulder at the screen.

The readouts indicated that they were approaching the first star system on the edge of the Kuriyar Cluster. It wasn't exactly on the line Harry Kim had plotted, but it was close, just a few light-hours to one side. There were eleven planets circling a G-type star—seven gas giants, two burned-out cinders too close to the primary for anything resembling humanoid life, and two fair-sized planets located in the habitable zone. Nothing was out of the ordinary in that.

The readings for the two in the habitable zone, however, were not ordinary at all. That was obvious even at a casual glance.

Somehow, she didn't think they were going to find any coffee plantations here.

"Mr. Kim," Janeway called without taking her eyes from the display, "I want you to run a full sensor scan on the third and fourth planets in that system ahead of us."

"Yes, Captain," Kim replied.

A moment later, still standing at the forward

console, Janeway studied the results of that sensor scan, frowning at what she saw.

Both planets might have been inhabited M-class worlds once. They weren't anymore.

The third planet's atmosphere was gone, stripped away completely. The rocky surface was boiling hot, seething with pools of radioactive lava. The heat did not come from the local sun, nor from normal volcanism; something had flash-fried the entire planet, burning away the atmosphere, and the planet had not yet cooled.

Theoretically, a massive asteroid bombardment could have been responsible, but most of the system was free of celestial debris—if there had once been asteroids, *all* of them had hit something. And the radiation wasn't anything that asteroid impacts would explain—not unless those asteroids were made up of some very peculiar elements.

And there were no traces of any such elements. In fact, there were no heavy elements present at all.

Something had blasted the third planet into this state, and Janeway knew of no natural phenomenon that would have left quite these conditions.

The fourth planet was not quite as bad. Although the planet's temperature was unnaturally high, the original surface was not completely obliterated. The atmosphere was still there, but it was a seething fog of radiation and corrosive poisons, totally inimical to carbon-based life.

The sensors detected structures that did not appear natural here and there on the fourth planet, but there was no sign of life anywhere on that entire world—not even so much as anaerobic bacteria.

"The war did this?" Janeway asked, turning to Neelix, who had come up beside her. "The P'nir, or the Hachai?"

"I don't know, Captain," the Talaxian replied. "I told you, no one comes here. But I would assume so."

Appalled, Janeway studied the sensor readouts again, and noticed something new.

Both planets were surrounded by clouds of orbiting wreckage—but there was something odd about the drifting debris. Janeway frowned, and checked the planetary scans again.

There were no metals.

The orbital wreckage was mostly organic—plastics, fabrics, and what were almost certainly corpses. The rest was lighter minerals. There were tons of organic material, but virtually no metal.

How could that be? Every starfaring species Janeway had ever heard of used metal to build their ships. If that wreckage didn't come from spaceships, where *did* it come from?

And if it came from spaceships, why wasn't there any metal left?

She looked at the reports on the planetary surfaces again. She had already noticed that there weren't any heavy elements, but now she looked more closely and realized just what that meant.

The planetary crusts had been stripped of every trace of useful metals.

The planetary cores were the usual nickel-iron,

and the star was young enough that the system should have been rich in heavy elements; the planets' crusts *should* have shown scattered deposits of iron, copper, lead, titanium . . .

The metals must have been there once.

They weren't now.

Even if the natural deposits had all been mined out to build the civilizations that had presumably once flourished here, the metals should have still been present somewhere, even if only in the form of slag.

"Where's all the metal?" she said aloud.

"Gone for warship hulls, most likely," Neelix said.

Janeway turned to stare at him.

"I told you, Captain," he said, "the Hachai and the P'nir have been fighting for a *long* time. They've stripped whole planets to build their fleets."

"And that orbiting debris?" Chakotay asked, stepping up to join the pair at the forward console.

"The remains of their defenses, I suppose," Neelix said. "I think this would have been a P'nir system; the P'nir are said to be fond of orbital fortresses."

"Those defenses don't seem to have worked," the First Officer remarked.

"Of course not," Neelix agreed. "*No* defense can hold out *forever* against a really determined attack. And the Hachai are pretty determined people."

"Of course not," Janeway said, appalled.

"Now, Captain," Neelix asked, his tone wheedling, "do you think we might change course, so as to not run into the Hachai fleet that *did* this?"

Janeway turned and looked across the bridge to Ensign Kim, behind his console in Ops. "When were these worlds destroyed?" she demanded.

"Just a minute, Captain," Kim said, as he studied the readings. Then he looked up. "Judging by the vacuum evaporation of the surface molecules from objects among the orbital debris," he said, "I'd estimate that the objects I picked as samples have been drifting untouched here for roughly two hundred standard years."

Janeway stared at Kim for a moment, then straightened and nodded. "I hardly think, Mr. Neelix," she said, "that any war fleet would still be in the area, looking for stragglers, after two centuries." She took another look at the viewscreen, at the image of the blackened ruins that had once been inhabited worlds, then stepped back and settled into her seat.

"I don't think anyone here was producing any tetryon beams, either."

"They'd be too busy fighting," Neelix replied. "Anyone anywhere in the Kuriyar Cluster would be. There's nothing here that's going to help."

"You don't know that," Janeway replied.

"But I knew that there was a war here, didn't I?" Neelix protested.

"Yes, you did," Janeway agreed, "but that doesn't mean there's nothing *but* a war. And in fact," she added, "I would guess that your war here is long since over. A conflict at that level of ferocity could not possibly have been sustained for so long."

Neelix looked at the screen.

"I hope you're right, Captain," he said. "I'd like to think so. But the war was still going on the last I heard."

CHAPTER
4

THE NEXT STAR SYSTEM THAT THE *VOYAGER* approached might have had a habitable planet orbiting it at one time; what it had now was an asteroid belt and three gas giants.

They weren't going to find any supplies here, either; that was obvious. And this time no one made any jokes about coffee plantations.

A quick analysis indicated that the asteroid field was not part of the system's original structure; a small planet had been destroyed to create it. By tracking orbital patterns, Harry Kim estimated that the destruction had taken place some three centuries before.

Whether the shattering of the planet had been

natural or whether a world had been deliberately smashed could not be determined. There was no sign of any inherent instability in the remaining fragments, but that didn't rule out a natural impact, or some sort of collapse.

An analysis of the core might have told them more, but the planet's metallic core was gone; the asteroids were all rock, presumably from the mantle or crust, and all without any trace of useful metals. A few chunks appeared to have once been part of a planetary surface; Janeway thought that she saw certain markings here and there that might even have been the remains of canals or highways.

"Take us in closer," she ordered, rising and stepping forward for a better view.

Paris obeyed; with shields raised to fend off any stray chunks of rock, the *Voyager* made its way cautiously into the asteroid belt.

"Was there anything in particular that you wanted to see?" Paris asked, when the ship was within the area where a planet had once orbited.

"Yes," Janeway said. *"That* one." She pointed at one of the chunks of rocky crust that seemed to have structures clinging to it. "The sensors say it's hollow."

"Hollow?" Paris looked at the readings, startled. "I don't show that here."

"It's not *completely* hollow," Janeway agreed, "but there are cavities in it, and I want a look at them. Match speeds with it, and take us down within transporter range."

"Aye-aye," Paris replied.

"Transporter range, Captain?" Chakotay asked, stepping up behind her.

Janeway nodded. "I want a look at whatever is inside that piece," she said. "I want to see if this really *was* an inhabited planet, and see if I can find some evidence about just what happened to it."

Chakotay frowned. "You're planning to beam over to the asteroid?"

"That's right."

"It may not be safe," Chakotay said. "Perhaps I should go, instead?"

Janeway shook her head. "No," she said. "I want to see for myself. Besides, Commander, you don't have the necessary scientific training. It'll be safe enough; I'll be in a spacesuit, and you'll be able to transport me back if there's any danger."

That was true enough about the training, Chakotay thought. Janeway had been a science officer before her promotion to captain, and knew more about astrophysics, exochemistry, and xenosociology than anyone else aboard the *Voyager*—certainly more than Chakotay did; his own background was far less technically oriented.

Still, he did not like the idea of the ship's captain undertaking such a venture.

"I would remind the captain," he said, "that we will be unable to maintain a transporter lock on you while our shields are up."

"We can turn the ship so that the stern is toward the asteroid," Janeway said, "and keep the forward and lateral shields up while lowering the aft shields, just as we would while docking a shuttlecraft. That will allow us full use of the transporter, and it's very unlikely that any chunk of celestial debris would come at us from that direction."

Chakotay reluctantly acknowledged that such a proposal ought to work.

"Good," Janeway said. "Commander, you have the conn. Mr. Kim, Mr. Tuvok, you're with me."

A few minutes later three spacesuited figures shimmered into existence on the surface of the asteroid. Harry Kim looked about while Tuvok began scanning the area with his tricorder.

The view was an odd one—the surface seemed as flat as that of a planet, rather than the jagged, uneven shape Harry had expected, but it cut off abruptly no more than a few kilometers away in every direction, as if they were standing atop a narrow plateau. And where from a plateau he might have seen more of the world spread out below, here there was nothing at all beyond the edge, nothing but the black of space and the clear light of the stars.

"Be careful, Mr. Kim," Janeway cautioned, as the three of them looked about. "Your legs are strong enough to push you right off into space when the gravity is this low."

"I know, Captain," Kim said. "We practiced low-gravity movement at the Academy."

Janeway nodded. "But at the Academy you had magnetic boots."

"But my spacesuit—aren't these boots . . ." Kim began, looking down, startled.

"They're magnetic, all right," Janeway said, "but

this asteroid isn't. There's no ferrous metal in it at all. So just move very, very carefully."

"Yes, ma'am," Kim agreed. "Um . . . Captain? If you wanted to see the inside of the asteroid, why did we beam down to the surface?"

"Because I want to see the surface, too, Ensign," Janeway explained, "and because if there's anything dangerous here, it's more likely to be in there than out here."

Kim nodded.

"Also," she added, "there's enough loose material in the cavity that transporting directly in might be difficult—you wouldn't want to arrive with something stuck inside you."

Kim could hardly argue with that.

"There would seem to be no question that this place was inhabited, Captain," Tuvok remarked, as he scanned about them with his tricorder.

That was obvious to all three of them.

They had materialized in a broad, shallow trench that had looked as if it might once have been a drainage ditch or perhaps a canal of some sort. As far as they had been able to see from the *Voyager* the trench might have been artificial, or might just have been an unusually regular natural feature.

From where they stood now, however, there was no longer any possible question. The trench was clearly artificial. Natural features were not edged with square blocks of dressed white stone with intricate and perfectly symmetrical decorative patterns carved into them.

"The planet was certainly inhabited at one

time," Janeway agreed. "The question is, was it still inhabited at the time of its destruction, or were its people already safely gone by then?" She swung her own tricorder about, scanning the area, and then pointed.

"That way," she said. "There's an opening that leads down into the cavity I want to investigate."

Together, moving very slowly and cautiously in the asteroid's feeble microgravity, the three moved along the shallow trench.

At last Janeway paused. "Under there," she said, pointing at an immense stone slab.

Kim blinked. "How are we going to move *that?*" he asked. "It must weigh tons!"

"On the contrary, Ensign," Tuvok replied, as he bent down and hooked his gloved fingers under the edge of the stone. "It *masses* tons; however, it *weighs* no more than a few hundred grams."

The Vulcan lifted, and the stone came up slowly—then spun off into space. Kim stepped back involuntarily, and watched as the slab sailed off toward the stars.

"I hope that's not going to hit the *Voyager,*" he said, as he watched the stone tumble away.

Tuvok said, "No, it will not. I would judge, from its present trajectory, that I have merely put it into orbit around the asteroid, and that it will curve around, missing the *Voyager* by several kilometers."

"Oh," Kim said, feeling a trifle foolish.

"It was a good point to raise, Mr. Kim," Janeway

assured him. "Come on." She pointed at the spot where the stone had lain.

The opening into the asteroid was rectangular, as clearly artificial as the decorative stonework. Kim stepped up to the edge and looked down.

"It's dark," he said.

Janeway turned on her wrist light and shone it down into the pit, revealing a stone shaft.

"And it's deep," Kim said. "How will we get down there? Are we going to use the transporter after all?"

"I don't think that will be necessary, Mr. Kim," Janeway said, as she stepped up on the rim of the opening and then stepped off, over the pit.

Kim watched, astonished, as Janeway gradually sank down into the pit.

"It seems clear, Mr. Kim," Tuvok said, "that you did not have enough practice in microgravity conditions at the Academy. If we ever return safely to the Federation, I shall inform Starfleet that this omission in the curriculum should be attended to."

Then he stepped up on the edge, turned on his wrist light, and stepped off, as Janeway had. He, too, sank slowly into the shaft.

They were falling, Kim knew—but falling very slowly in the asteroid's tiny gravity. As Janeway had warned him, the danger here wasn't in falling, it was in drifting away from the asteroid entirely.

Taking a deep breath, Kim stepped up on the rim, as his superior officers had done, and stepped out into the empty space above the shaft.

As Janeway and Tuvok had, he began to drift slowly downward, into the pit.

The sensation was very odd; it did not feel like falling. Instead, it simply felt as if he had gone from low gravity to zero gravity. However, he could see the walls of the shaft moving past, more and more quickly as he fell—though still slowly.

He was falling no faster than he might have walked when he landed on the bottom—and bounced.

Tuvok and Janeway caught him before he could drift more than a meter or so back up the shaft, and pulled him carefully back down. A moment later the three of them were standing on solid ground—though not as securely as Kim might have liked—and shining their lights around.

The original purpose of this shaft and the chamber at the bottom was not obvious; Kim supposed it might have been a disposal shaft, or for storage of some sort, or even a bomb shelter. Whatever it had been built for, the room at the bottom of the shaft was now simply a space cluttered with debris.

"What are we looking for, Captain?" he asked.

"That," Janeway said sadly.

Kim swung his own light around to where Janeway's beam pointed.

"Oh," he said.

They were huddled in one corner, half-buried under rubble. There were three of them, a large one and two small ones. The large one was roughly Kim's own size, though shorter and rounder, while the others were perhaps half as big.

They were shriveled and gray, mummified by long exposure to vacuum, but they had obviously been living creatures once; each had a head and four arms. Their legs, if they had any, were hidden under the wreckage. They didn't seem to have had any eyes, Kim thought at first, and then he reconsidered—those things on their heads that he had at first taken for antennae really looked more like eyestalks.

"It would seem that the planet *was* still inhabited when it was destroyed," Janeway said.

Tuvok scanned the pitiful little corpses with his tricorder, and said, "These creatures do appear to have died as a result of the planet's destruction, Captain—the dates and the manner of their death are consistent with that hypothesis. However, we cannot be sure that these were intelligent beings, rather than lesser indigenous fauna."

Janeway reached down and picked something from the hand of the smallest of the mummies.

"Can't we?" she said. She held out the object.

It was a bit of fabric, sewn and stuffed into a specific and recognizable form.

A doll, in the shape of one of the four-armed, eyestalked aliens. It wore a tiny shirt that bore a decorative design, stitched into the fabric—a design identical to one of those on the stones they had seen on the surface of the asteroid.

"Animals don't make toys in their own likeness, Mr. Tuvok," Janeway said.

"Indeed," the Vulcan replied.

Kim looked at the little rag doll, then back at the

mummies, and he shuddered inside his spacesuit. The situation was clear. A parent and two children had taken shelter, and had been trapped in here when the end came, and now they were still here, dead for three centuries. . . .

"We've seen what I wanted to see," Janeway said. She tapped her combadge. "Three to beam up."

Fifteen minutes later the three of them were back on the bridge of the *Voyager,* the alien doll still in Janeway's hand. She looked it over.

It was brittle and on the verge of turning to powder; three centuries in hard vacuum had boiled away every trace of any sort of fluid or moisture the fabric had ever contained. Already, one of the four rolled-cloth arms had come off and both the tiny eyestalks, which had been made of some sort of stiffened thread, had disintegrated. The two stubby legs were jammed up into the rounded base of the doll, but that was how they had been to begin with—it wasn't anything that the long exposure to space had done.

"Mr. Neelix," she said, "do you recognize this species?" She held out the toy.

Neelix studied it without touching it.

"It looks something like a Hachai," the Talaxian said. "If it had those two little things on its head, with eyes on the end . . ."

"It did," Janeway said, pulling the doll back and looking down at it for a long moment.

It was blue-gray in color, darker but otherwise not too unlike the color of the *Voyager*'s interior walls, and she wondered whether that was its original hue, or whether the dyes in the fabric had been damaged by vacuum—or by something else, before that, when its owner was still alive. She remembered a few dog toys that had started out some bright color and been reduced to muddy browns or grays in fairly short order.

She smiled at the memory of those well-chewed toys, but the smile vanished quickly.

This hadn't been a dog's toy; it had been a child's. That child had wound up dead.

The mummies had been gray, but they had been covered with dust.

Then she looked up at the viewscreen, at the panorama of asteroids that had once been a planet. "So that was a Hachai world?" she asked. "And the P'nir destroyed it?"

"I would assume so," Neelix said.

Janeway nodded thoughtfully, and set the doll carefully aside.

"Mr. Paris," she said, "take us out of this system, on a heading of eight four mark three-seven."

"But that's straight on into the heart of the cluster," Neelix said.

"Yes, of course," Janeway replied.

"But that's . . . that's where the P'nir are!" the Talaxian protested.

"If there still are any P'nir, Mr. Neelix," Janeway agreed, "then yes, they're probably somewhere ahead of us."

"Captain," Neelix said, "do you *really* want to risk running into people who could do this?"

"Three hundred years ago they might have been able to blow up planets," Janeway replied. "That doesn't mean they can do it now. And that tetryon beam came from somewhere in this direction."

Neelix threw up his hands in disgust at that.

"Warp one, Mr. Paris," Janeway said.

CHAPTER
5

JANEWAY LEANED HER HEAD BACK AGAINST THE smooth gray fabric of her command chair as the *Voyager* neared the next system. "Slow to impulse," she said. "We'll take a look here."

"Do we have to?" Neelix muttered, as he clutched the railing behind her. "If you insist on traveling through this cluster, I wish you'd at least do it quicker."

Janeway glanced up at him.

"There's nothing alive around here, Captain," Neelix said, leaning over the rail and peering down at her. "Nothing except for the P'nir and the Hachai, anyway, and you're not going to get any supplies from *them.*"

Janeway turned away, glancing toward the Operations station. "Scan the area, Mr. Kim," she said, ignoring the Talaxian. "Take your time."

"Captain," Chakotay protested, leaning over from his own seat, "I'm beginning to agree with Neelix."

Janeway looked at him in surprise.

"I don't mean about leaving the Kuriyar Cluster, or deciding to come here in the first place," Chakotay explained, "but is it really necessary to investigate every system we pass along the way?"

"I think it is," Janeway replied. "We're looking for something, Commander—had you forgotten? Whatever it was that produced that tetryon beam might have come from one of these systems."

"It wasn't *in* any of them at the time we were scanned," Chakotay pointed out. "Why would it be now?"

"Because it isn't out here in the interstellar void," Janeway said. "If it *was* around here, then either it's gone completely, or it's moved into one of these systems and is lost in the clutter."

"Or it may be farther up ahead," Chakotay said, "and by taking time to explore each system we pass we may be letting it get away."

"We may be," Janeway said. "Sometimes we have to make choices on the basis of partial information, Commander, and whichever one we make may prove to be wrong. I prefer to at least take a quick look at each system we pass." She glanced down at the crumbling remains of the Hachai doll, a blue-gray lump on the smooth gray panel beside her chair. "If we don't find what we're looking for in any of them, at least we might learn more about the Hachai and the P'nir, and anything we can learn about them might be useful if and when we actually encounter those war fleets Neelix keeps warning us about."

Chakotay's lips tightened; then he straightened up and turned away.

"Stay on course for the inner system, Mr. Paris," Janeway said—but as she spoke she was watching Chakotay.

She hadn't expected his outburst. Perhaps the strain of their situation was getting to him; certainly, the officers and crew had reason for low morale.

Still, she wouldn't have thought Chakotay would object to their brief side trips. Usually, despite his lack of scientific training, he was almost as interested in exploration and discovery as she was.

Perhaps Neelix's constant warnings were getting on the first officer's nerves.

"Mr. Kim," she called, "tell me about the system."

"It's a class-K star, Captain," Kim reported. "Ten planets—two of the inner ones are coorbital. The coorbitals are just airless rock; the third one shows a runaway greenhouse effect, like Venus. The outer five are ringed gas giants—no carbon-based life possible. Should I scan them all for methane-breathers?"

"Don't bother," Janeway said. "Not unless

someone there is building spacecraft." She turned to Neelix. "The P'nir aren't methane-breathers, are they?"

The Talaxian shook his head. "The Hachai and the P'nir are both carbon-based," Neelix told her, "and they're all you'll find in this cluster."

Janeway nodded, then turned her attention back to the Ops station.

"What can you tell me about the fourth and fifth planets?" she asked.

"The fifth one looks pretty dead," Kim reported. "There's an atmosphere, but it's thin, not much oxygen. The only moisture seems to be in the polar ice caps, and those are both frozen solid with a mix of water ice and carbon dioxide."

"Sounds cold and nasty," Neelix remarked.

"Cold and nasty just about describes it," Kim agreed.

"And the fourth planet?" Janeway asked.

"It's on the far side of the primary right now, so the readings aren't . . ." Kim began. Then he stopped speaking and stared at the screen.

"We're picking up life-form readings," he said.

Chakotay, who had been staring moodily at Tuvok and the Security/Tactical station, turned abruptly, focusing his attention on Kim instead.

"What sort of life-forms?" Janeway asked, startled—and pleased. She got to her feet and stepped up to the forward console, to one side of the helm, to check the screen there.

She had begun to think that the entire cluster was totally lifeless, that anything that had ever lived there was long dead, wiped out by the Hachai-P'nir war. She had seen nothing to back up Neelix's belief that the war was still going on; the two systems they had visited before this one were completely bereft of life, and there were no indications anywhere of continued activity. They had found no ion trails or energy traces, or any other evidence that starships were still cruising this region of space.

Life-form readings from the fourth planet were totally unexpected—but welcome.

And the life-form readings were there, all right—the signal descriptions stretched across the black screen in lines of glowing golden type.

Of course, if those life-forms down there were either P'nir or Hachai, they might be armed and hostile. The war just *might* still be going on.

"Shields up," she ordered, glancing over to starboard, where Tuvok manned his station. Then she looked up at the main viewscreen. "Take us in for a closer look, Mr. Paris, but don't do anything foolish—Mr. Neelix may be right about the war after all."

"Aye-aye," Paris replied. "Ahead one-quarter impulse, on heading two-four-seven mark thirteen."

The planet grew from a distant speck to a blue-white globe that filled most of the main viewer. Sensors detected no orbital fortresses here, intact or otherwise; there were no signs of defenses of any kind.

There were also no traces to show that spaceships had ever before visited or left this world; if these were Hachai or P'nir, they were no longer actively involved in any interstellar war—not unless it was fought with weapons and methods unlike anything Janeway had ever heard of.

That settled, the *Voyager*'s sensors were directed at the planet itself.

There were cities—or fair-sized towns, at any rate—and roads connecting them, but the civilization on the planet, such as it was, appeared to be rather primitive. The sensors showed no indication of mechanization. Not only were there no spaceships, there were no aircraft, no electrical fields, no subspace emissions, no radio transmissions.

Janeway considered that information, and decided not to go close enough for a more detailed visual scan. They had no urgent business here, and the Prime Directive forbade interfering with the local cultures; besides, a visual scan hardly seemed necessary, given the readings. The society here was clearly largely pretechnological.

A reason for that was also clear—no metals could be detected anywhere in the planetary crust. That was sufficiently anomalous to be listed in flashing red on the sensor readout.

"Is this whole *cluster* metal-depleted?" Janeway wondered aloud.

"I don't know," Chakotay replied, as he studied a display on the flipped-up panel by his chair, "but you might want to take a look at grid sector 63-24 north."

Janeway noticed that Chakotay was sounding

more enthusiastic now. She tapped keys to shift her own readings to the location he had indicated, and sure enough, there was a significant amount of metal, right there on the surface, hard to miss—iron, copper, titanium. . . .

This metal was not in a natural deposit, though—it was an artificial structure. The metals had been processed, separated, and incorporated into a construction of some sort.

"What is that?" she asked. She pondered the readings for a moment, and then decided that a visual scan was called for after all. "Mr. Kim," she ordered, "give me a better look at that structure."

"Telescopic scan working, Captain," Kim replied. "Onscreen."

A moment later Janeway stepped forward, hands clasped behind her back, and considered the image the scanners presented.

"It's a ship," she said. "It has to be."

It was bulbous, alien in design—but it did appear to be a spaceship.

Or part of one.

"Someone must have crashed there," Paris said.

"It looks more as if they were building it," Chakotay said, getting to his feet and pointing. "See those wooden towers around it? That looks like construction scaffolding."

"But there's no one around," Janeway said. "It's abandoned."

"Hull corrosion would seem to indicate that it's been abandoned for a long time," Kim confirmed. "Fifty or sixty years, at least."

"They ran out of metal," Neelix said, leaning over the rail behind Janeway and Chakotay. "That's a Hachai design; they were building it there, and they ran out of metal and couldn't finish it."

Janeway stared at the screen for a long moment. She tried to imagine the four-armed, stalk-eyed, rounded little creatures building warships.

Maybe they did—but they weren't building anymore. She turned away.

"Maybe they did run out of metal," she said. "At any rate, no one here has been putting out any tetryon beams recently. No one's fighting any wars, either, and whatever they're doing, it's no concern of ours. Take us back out of the system, Mr. Paris—warp two."

CHAPTER
6

THE NEXT SYSTEM, A LIGHT-HOUR OUT OF THEIR PATH, had fourteen planets; the sixth had once been habitable but was now bare, lifeless rock, stripped of its atmosphere—and of its metals.

Janeway and Chakotay watched the main viewscreen wordlessly from their seats as the *Voyager* passed over that broad expanse of utter desolation.

When they had seen what little there was to see, Janeway ordered, "Take us out." She slumped in her chair.

"Aye-aye," Paris replied, and the image on the screen began to withdraw.

"When we found that that last system was still inhabited," Chakotay said quietly, leaning over toward the captain, "I'd hoped that it was a good sign, that we'd find more. Those first two systems, those three destroyed worlds . . . those saddened me. Seeing those ruins ate at my spirit."

Janeway glanced at him.

He met her gaze.

"Yes, that was why I objected to visiting the third," he said. "I didn't want to see any more of death, devastation, and destruction." He pointed at the Hachai doll. "That toy you brought back with you brought it home to me—these were *people* who lived on these worlds, people fighting and dying out here, people who might have worn different shapes than ours, but people with *spirits* like ours, with families and loved ones. The child who owned that doll had died, probably without ever knowing why, and certainly without deserving such a hideous death. This war of theirs destroyed millions, perhaps billions, of people on both sides—and for what? It's even more senseless than the Cardassian imperialism—from what Neelix said, no one even *knows* why these people were fighting!"

"It happens," Janeway said. "You've seen war before. You've fought, yourself."

"I know," Chakotay said. "But to have the entire Hachai and P'nir civilizations destroyed, both their races completely wiped out . . ."

"There were still survivors in the third system," Janeway said.

"There were people there," Chakotay said, "but we don't know for certain they were survivors; we didn't get a good look at them, to see if they were the same as that doll. They might have been some other species entirely, one that wasn't involved in the war." He straightened up.

"I *hope* they were survivors," he said. "Maybe, if they are, they've learned something. Maybe they'll rebuild, someday, and venture off their planet into space, and maybe this time they won't make the same mistakes."

Janeway shook her head. "They don't have any metals to work with," she said. "They'll probably never be able to leave that planet."

Chakotay didn't reply.

"Even if they never leave, never rebuild their lost technology, it's a better fate than *that,*" Janeway said, pointing at the viewer, where the barren surface of the sixth planet gleamed dully in the light of its sun.

Chakotay nodded. He could hardly argue with that.

And right now he didn't feel like arguing with anything—except perhaps whatever gods or spirits ruled this cluster, yet had allowed such a catastrophe.

As they left the fourth system and its blasted sixth planet behind, Janeway stepped up to the forward console and consulted the *Voyager*'s star charts; ahead of them lay an empty stretch. The four systems they had passed through were in an outlying arm of the Kuriyar Cluster, and ahead lay the cluster's heart, but for the moment they faced several light-years of empty nothingness.

Janeway looked at that emptiness and felt suddenly tired.

At first she thought that the devastation was getting to her, but then she realized that she had been on the bridge almost constantly for the past eleven hours. Some part of her mind was telling her that this was her chance to rest, that her crew could manage without her for a while. There were no more star systems to investigate for a dozen light-years.

"Commander," she said, "take the bridge; I'm going to get some rest."

"Aye-aye, Captain," Chakotay said.

As Janeway left the bridge she saw that Chakotay had settled into his chair, his face and body seeming to sag—he was probably tired, as well.

The last thing she saw of the bridge, as the door of the turbolift closed, was her first officer picking up the fragile, crumbling Hachai doll, and slowly turning it over and over in his hands.

CHAPTER
7

JANEWAY WOKE SUDDENLY, UNSURE JUST WHAT HAD brought her out of her sleep; she had been dreaming of home, of Mark and of her dog, and it had turned into a nightmare where she found them both mummified in an ancient tunnel. Now she was staring up at the stars through the sloping windows over her bed, back aboard the *Voyager,* among surroundings that were becoming a little *too* familiar.

"Captain Janeway to the bridge," the speaker at the head of her bed repeated.

"On my way," she said, swinging her feet to the floor.

She glanced at a clock and frowned. Unless

Chakotay had ordered an increase in speed—a *major* increase in speed—they should still be in the void between star systems. Why would she be needed?

She didn't like to think about what might be responsible for interrupting her rest.

She hesitated for a moment; the call hadn't expressed any great urgency. In an emergency she would have headed straight to the bridge in her nightgown, but as it was, she thought she could spare a few seconds to get back into uniform.

"Lights," she ordered.

"What is it?" she asked, as she stepped out of the turbolift a moment later.

"Sorry to wake you, Captain," Chakotay said, turning to face her. He was standing in the very center of the bridge, behind Lieutenant Paris's shoulder. "A few minutes ago we entered a large, unusually dense dust cloud." He gestured at the main viewscreen, where bands of shadow obscured most of the stars. "It's mostly made up of particles of ionized metals—maybe it's where all the metal in this cluster went. At any rate, the cloud density is increasing, and I'd have called you soon anyway, but when we got a little way into it the sensors spotted something ahead that I thought you'd want to see immediately."

Janeway nodded and looked at the viewscreen as she stepped down to the central level. Thanks to the dust there was nothing much to see on the viewer; she turned to a computer display on the forward console.

The sensors, able to look through the dust cloud, told a different story. There was something ahead of them, all right—something strange. It was registering on every sort of sensor, but none of the readings made sense.

For a few seconds she studied those readings silently, trying to see a pattern or logic to them, but nothing revealed itself. "What *is* that?" she said at last.

"I don't know," Chakotay replied. He frowned and stared at the screen, even though the anomaly didn't show there except as an occasional glimpse of something that could have been an ordinary star or nebula. "It's still too distant to say, and the dust cloud badly distorts our data. It's huge, though, whatever it is, and its energy output is comparable to the Caretaker's Array. It's too stable to be a plasma storm, and besides, its output isn't like any plasma storm I ever heard of before. And it's directly ahead of us, on the line that Ensign Kim plotted; assuming it hasn't moved, either that thing produced the tetryon beam, or the beam passed directly through it."

"It's not generating any tetryon radiation now," Janeway pointed out.

"No," Chakotay agreed, "but it's generating just about everything else."

That was true, as Janeway could see for herself; whatever it was ahead of them, it was radiating all up and down the electromagnetic spectrum, pouring out incredible amounts of energy.

The energy emissions weren't steady, though; the

thing's output fluctuated wildly, with no pattern that Janeway could see. At one instant light and heat would be spraying out, at the next the thing, whatever it was, would go dark—relatively dark, at any rate; the output never went anywhere near zero. Gamma radiation flickered and flared; radio, microwaves, infrared, ultraviolet, and charged particles scattered from it, dancing in all directions and skipping wildly up and down the spectrum, diffracting through the dust cloud that surrounded both the object and the *Voyager*. The bar graphs on the display bounced up and down like so many hyperactive kittens.

The Array had pulsed with energy, almost like a heartbeat; this thing was sputtering like a roman candle.

"Maybe the companion is in trouble," Paris suggested. It was obvious to anyone that this sort of output wasn't normal or healthy.

"Maybe it's not the companion," Janeway replied. "Maybe it's something else entirely."

"But, Captain," Kim protested from his station, "what else could be throwing around that sort of power?"

"I don't know," Janeway said. She glanced at Chakotay, who shrugged.

"Your guess is as good as mine," the first officer said. "The energy signature isn't anything like the Array's—but it isn't like anything else, either. Not even itself; notice how it changes?"

"Any idea what that means?"

Chakotay shrugged again.

"It's *got* to be the Caretaker's companion," Kim said.

"We have insufficient data to choose any one hypothesis," Tuvok remarked.

Janeway glanced up at Neelix, who was still there, now standing well aft at the primary ship's-status display.

"I never saw anything quite like it before," the little alien admitted. "But I could make a guess . . ."

"So could we," Janeway said, cutting him off. "If that's all you can say about it, then I'll thank you to stay quiet for the moment, Mr. Neelix." She took her seat and called, "Bridge to Engineering."

"Torres here," came the reply.

"We're reading something ahead, B'Elanna, something very large and energetic," Janeway said. "We're pretty sure it's a construct of some kind, not a natural phenomenon. Assuming someone built it, we'd be interested in your opinion of what they might have built it *for.*"

"I'll take a look," came the reply.

Down in the engineering section, B'Elanna Torres had been cheerfully immersed in fine-tuning the *Voyager*'s warp core. After years of making do with whatever decrepit equipment the Maquis could beg, borrow, or steal, it was a delight to get her hands on Starfleet's latest model, even one that had gotten banged up by the Caretaker's displacement wave.

Machines, she knew, didn't look at her warily because she was half-Klingon and known for her temper. She found them much easier to deal with than people. And a modern warp drive was so wonderfully delicate and complex—she could easily have spent months or years tinkering with it, getting it tuned to the absolute peak of efficiency.

The outside world wasn't about to let her have those months, though; the *Voyager'*s chief engineer had plenty of other duties to attend to.

This particular interruption was annoying, but it wasn't until she had switched on the nearest available display that it struck Torres just how odd it was.

Since when did the captain, herself a top-notch science officer, need help in identifying anything?

Torres hadn't thought about that when she gave her initial response; she had still been thinking about core pressures and resonance frequencies. Now, though, she took a look at the screen and muttered, "What the hell is *that?*" And although she didn't say so aloud, she did wonder why in the galaxy Kathryn Janeway thought she, B'Elanna Torres, might do a better job of identifying it than anyone on the bridge.

She began scanning the readings, and then she thought she understood.

That thing out there wasn't anything a scientist could be expected to identify. Science dealt with the natural universe, and the object ahead did not look natural at all. Science made *sense,* and that thing out there, with its wild discharges of energy, didn't.

Engineering made sense too, of course—but

sometimes the sense wasn't immediately obvious. Engineering dealt with the *created* universe, rather than the natural one, and sometimes sentients created the damnedest contraptions.

Torres liked to think she was pretty good at puzzling out contraptions, even unlikely ones, but that thing ahead had her stumped. She studied the readings and tried to make sense of them.

For a long moment, as Torres studied and the captain waited, the bridge was silent save for the soft hum of the engines and the faint beeps and chirps of equipment performing its proper functions. No one spoke; the soft shuffling of black-clad feet on gray carpet made no sound.

At the rear of the bridge Neelix glanced unhappily from one officer to another, obviously eager to speak, but he restrained himself; he knew he had irritated the captain, and that to argue now would irritate her more.

"Captain, we've got a better reading on its size now," Kim said, breaking the silence. "And . . . well, it's really *immense*. Much bigger than the Array—it's hundreds of thousands of kilometers across. Usually. The size keeps shifting, as if it were expanding and contracting."

"Engineering to bridge," Torres's voice said, before Janeway could respond. "Captain, I don't know what it's for, but if these readings are accurate and that thing out there is a machine doing what it was designed to do, its designers are insane. It's either deliberately wasteful and destructive, or the worst piece of engineering I've ever seen."

"Do you think it could have been built by the Caretaker's companion?" Janeway asked.

"No," Torres replied immediately. "The Array was wasteful, but it wasn't *sloppy*. This design, if it *is* a design, isn't anything like the Array."

The bridge crew exchanged glances.

Tuvok cleared his throat. Janeway turned her head to the right to look up at him.

"Captain," he said, "I would remind you that we are well inside what was at one time, and what may still be, a war zone. Perhaps this . . . thing ahead of us is directly related to that conflict?"

Neelix nodded eagerly, started to speak, then glanced around and thought better of it.

"Of course it is," Janeway said. She frowned at how slow she had been to recognize the obvious; perhaps she wasn't as fully awake as she ought to be. Insane and destructive, Torres had said . . . what else could it be but a war machine? It might even be whatever had shattered that planet three systems back, the one where she had found the Hachai doll.

She should have seen that immediately. She had been too focused on the *Voyager*'s own situation, on the central problem that faced them all— getting home. She had been thinking about that thing ahead in terms of whether it got them closer to that goal, rather than looking at it objectively and seeing it for what it was.

She couldn't allow that. That was wishful thinking, to look at everything as a potential shortcut back to the Alpha Quadrant, and wishful thinking was dangerous.

And their guide had been trying to tell her that all along, had been telling her that she was flying the *Voyager* into danger. Maybe it was time she listened.

She turned to her Talaxian guide, who had moved slightly to one side, trying to stay out of the way of one of the crewmen.

"Mr. Neelix," she said, "tell me more about the Hachai and the P'nir."

"Captain?" Neelix hurried to the railing and looked down at her.

"You heard me," Janeway said. "I want to know everything you can tell me about the inhabitants of this cluster."

Neelix gaped at her in surprise, then snapped his mouth shut.

Everything?

These Federation people had never before wanted to hear everything he knew about *anything;* usually they seemed to want him to shut up. He looked about the bridge at the other officers, to make sure they weren't preparing to laugh at him for some reason, then turned his attention back to the captain. "Why, I hardly know where to begin!" he said.

"Well, why not start off with a comparison?" Janeway suggested. "For example, which of them has the more advanced technology? Do you know? Would either of them be capable of building a weapon that size?" She pointed at the displays at the Ops station.

Neelix immediately saw that she didn't really want to know *everything* about the Hachai or the P'nir; his explanations of how to use Hachai funerary customs in salvage-rights negotiations, or the P'nir code of honor as applied to starship repair, would have to wait until some other time. What Captain Janeway really wanted, now that they had come across something other than blasted ruins or harmless primitives, was information about what to expect up ahead.

Neelix started to reply with a stream of warnings about the incredible power of Hachai and P'nir weaponry, but then he caught himself. He didn't want to annoy anyone, or amuse anyone, by exaggerating, and besides, these people had already seen those ruined worlds. Exaggeration wasn't needed, and he wanted the captain to *listen*. He looked at the clouds of dust on the main viewer and weighed his words carefully before he spoke, and then kept himself, as much as he could, to the exact, unadorned truth.

"Their technologies were always pretty evenly balanced," he said. "After all, how else could their war drag on so long? Even if it's over now, as you seem to believe, it lasted for centuries."

Janeway nodded. "Go on," she said.

Neelix thought for a moment, planning out his words, then said, "Well, both sides were said to be masters of defensive technology—before the supply finally ran out outside this cluster, the Hachai shield generators were always in great demand, a very profitable item whenever you could get hold of one." He smiled in fond recollection. He liked profitable merchandise.

He was about to say more when Janeway interrupted him. "Were the Hachai shields better than the P'nir shields?" she asked.

"Not really, but you couldn't *get* P'nir shields," Neelix explained. "Not so far back as I've ever heard, anyway—certainly not in my lifetime."

"Could either of them have built something like that?" Janeway gestured at the displays.

Neelix hesitated, then admitted, "I don't know. I'm not sure I understand your readings. . . ."

"We're through enough of the dust cloud to be within visual range of the object now, Captain," Kim reported, interrupting the Talaxian.

"Onscreen," Janeway said.

The viewer lit up with coruscating waves of color, too bright to look at safely. Janeway raised an arm, shielding her eyes.

"Filter that down," she snapped.

The glare vanished, revealing a rounded, irregular mass that seemed to be made up of swirling dots of polychrome light and shadow. It shifted shape constantly, like a gigantic amoeba, and a fine mist of debris seemed to be emanating from it, spreading slowly out in all directions and blending seamlessly into the dust cloud.

"How big *is* that?" Janeway asked.

The screen immediately displayed a scale, indicating that the mass was approximately two hundred and fifty thousand kilometers across—the size of a small star.

"Mr. Neelix," Janeway said, without turning to look at him, "to the best of your knowledge, could the P'nir or the Hachai build something the size of a star?"

"No," Neelix said, shaking his head sharply. "At least, I don't *think* so." He stared at the screen, trying to make sense of what he saw there. "But then, all that metal must have gone *somewhere. . . .*"

"Is that thing just a *machine?*" Paris asked. "It looks alive!"

"What's its mass?" Janeway asked. The computer promptly posted a sensor readout down one side of the main viewscreen; upon seeing the figures, Janeway frowned.

"It's not any ordinary machine," she said. "For an object that size, with that mass, its density would be lower than most gases."

"Perhaps it's hollow?" Paris suggested, glancing back over his shoulder.

"Perhaps it is not *one* machine, but *many,*" Tuvok suggested from behind his console. "I believe we have misjudged what we are seeing; I do not believe it to be a single object at all."

"Increase magnification. Enhance the image," Janeway ordered.

The blob expanded to fill the screen, and the bridge crew stared in stunned silence as it became obvious that Tuvok was quite right.

The mass was not a single object at all; it was

made up of many, many smaller objects, each of them moving independently, each maneuvering around the others. Energy fields surrounded each object, sometimes colliding with each other, and beams of energy flashed back and forth between them.

The objects were ships—thousands upon thousands of starships.

"They're gigantic," Paris said, awed.

"The smallest one I can read is about the size of a Galaxy-class starship," Chakotay observed, as he stepped forward to read the latest sensor reports. "The big ones—well, I've seen moons that were smaller."

"But what are they *doing?*" Harry Kim asked, staring at the screen. "Why are they bunched so close? Why are there so *many* of them? Why aren't they going anywhere?"

"I would have thought that was obvious, Ensign," Janeway said, as she, too, stared at the screen. "They're fighting. We've found the war, and where all the metal in this benighted cluster went."

CHAPTER
8

THE *VOYAGER* HUNG IN SPACE, DEEP WITHIN THE cloud of ionized metal dust, virtually motionless and safely out of range of the thousands of weapons being fired a few light-seconds away.

The *Voyager* waited, and while she waited, her crew watched. Paris remained at the helm, Kim at Ops, Tuvok at Security; Janeway and Chakotay occupied the two command chairs. Neelix and Kes stood, observing, Neelix now down by Janeway's left hand and Kes back by the starboard turbolift.

The Hachai doll had fallen to dust when someone had inadvertently bumped against it; all that remained was a smear of greasy dust on the platform beside Janeway's chair, dark gray on light.

Janeway started to reach for the doll, then remembered that it was gone. She looked down at the smudge, then back up at the viewer.

What she saw there made no immediate, obvious sense. To the unaided human eye the visual display on the bridge's main viewscreen was a seething, flickering, incomprehensible mass of fire and shadow.

To the ship's tactical officer, aided by his sensors and computers, it was something else entirely.

"I count approximately two thousand operational warships that I would describe as either dreadnoughts or heavy cruisers, all of them larger than anything in Starfleet," Tuvok reported, studying his displays. "There are also several thousand smaller vessels caught up in the conflict, ranging from the size of a Galaxy-class cruiser down to that of a runabout, and I observe large quantities of macroscopic wreckage in the area that would seem to indicate that both fleets were once considerably more numerous." He turned away from his screens to address Janeway directly across his console.

"I would estimate, Captain," he said, "that the resources of roughly fifteen hundred M-class planets would be required to build and maintain these fleets—in short, the total industrial output of this entire cluster."

"*Thousands* of warships?" Janeway glanced at the screen, then back at the Vulcan. "That's almost as incredible as one star-sized machine!"

"You said the industrial output of this entire cluster," Chakotay said.

"Yes, Commander."

"This cluster hasn't *got* any industrial output!" Chakotay exclaimed.

"Unfortunately true," the Vulcan replied calmly. "However, I worked on the assumption of a level of technology roughly equivalent to our own, reasonably organized and distributed, and working itself to the point of its own destruction to produce these fleets."

"How could they *maintain* such fleets, then?" Janeway asked. "If they destroyed their whole industrial base in building them . . ."

"I would say, Captain," Tuvok said, "that they did not so much destroy their industrial base as consume it, transferring it entirely to the fleets. The larger vessels here would appear to be fully self-contained and self-maintained—that, combined with the need for maximum firepower, explains their immense size."

"Then you think these fleets are all that's left of the Hachai and P'nir technologies?" Janeway asked.

"Indeed," Tuvok said. "That would appear to be the case."

Janeway turned and stared at the main screen.

"Incidentally, Captain," Tuvok continued, "it would appear that the dust cloud surrounding us, and extending for several million kilometers in all directions, is emanating from the battle. The cloud is made up of gases and particulate matter from destroyed or damaged ships. The density increases with proximity to the battle, and within the battle itself the density is sufficient to significantly interfere with our sensors; that, combined with the interlocking energy fields of the defensive shields, was why our initial readings indicated a single construct."

"Particulate matter?" Kes asked. She was watching everything with intense interest.

"Dust," Janeway told her.

"Metallic dust, ice crystals, and several other substances, including two varieties of what I take to be circulatory fluid," Tuvok explained.

"You mean blood," Chakotay said.

"Or ichor, yes," the Vulcan confirmed.

"Hachai and P'nir, presumably," Janeway said.

"Presumably," Tuvok agreed.

Kes shivered, and looked uneasily at the viewer. "We're inside a cloud of blood?" she asked.

"Yes," Tuvok said flatly.

Janeway looked at the vast, incredibly complex pattern of moving ships, weapons fire, and flaring shields, and asked, "Can you tell who's winning?"

"At the moment, Captain," the Vulcan replied, "neither side is winning."

"You mean it's a draw? A stalemate?" Janeway turned to look at the Vulcan.

"If by that you mean that no winner will ever emerge, then no, that is not necessarily the case," Tuvok replied. "If this battle is fought to a conclusion without outside interference and without any major change in the tactics employed, there should indeed be a victor, at least in a technical sense. There is every indication that the combatants intend to continue to an end, rather than withdrawing or negotiating. Therefore, an eventual winner can be expected, and in that sense, it is not a stalemate."

"Well, then, *which* side will win?" Janeway asked. "Can you tell?"

"Regrettably, Captain, I cannot," the Vulcan admitted. "I have only begun to analyze the battle formations, which are staggeringly intricate—so intricate that they form a system where major disruptions in one time and place might be absorbed without significantly affecting the whole, while elsewhere a single minor change could alter the entire course of the conflict. Above a certain level of complexity such systems cannot be reliably predicted with the resources we have aboard this ship."

"You can't even offer us odds?"

"The odds, Captain, would be fifty-fifty. It is already quite clear that as Mr. Neelix told us, the two sides are very evenly matched—so evenly that the loss of a single ship in the right time or place could determine the outcome. And in a battle as hard-fought as this, a ship could be lost to a single crew error or equipment failure at any time. There is no way to predict such a happenstance—but if the battle continues long enough, it is a statistical certainty that such an event will occur eventually."

"And when it does," Janeway said, "when that random ship is lost, the other side will capitalize on it—and win."

"Not a *random* ship, Captain," Tuvok corrected her. "The loss would need to happen at the right time and place. Otherwise, the damaged side will adjust, regroup, and wait, and perhaps the next time it will be the other side that suffers. It is only if the loss is at one of the crucial points of the battle that a single such event would be fatal."

Janeway nodded. "A chaotic system, you mean—where any one event could get lost in the noise, but the *right* event could trigger a cascade that would change everything."

"Exactly."

Janeway frowned thoughtfully.

"Suppose that that event never happens?" she asked. "Chaotic systems can be quite stable at times."

"If nothing happens to change the balance," Tuvok said, "I would estimate that this conflict will continue until all ships on both sides run out of power. Whichever side is still able to maneuver when the other has totally exhausted its resources will emerge victorious—but I am unable to determine which side that would be."

Janeway nodded. "And at the present rates of fire, how long do you think this state of exhaustion would take to occur?"

"You understand, of course, that due to the debris cloud and the shields, I have only very imprecise readings on most of those ships, Captain, and can therefore do no more than make a rough estimate."

"Estimate, then."

"Both sides seem to be using matter-antimatter reactors even though they show no signs of warp drive capability, and both also appear to have backup fission/fusion power systems that could, should they choose to do so, use the cloud of drifting wreckage as fuel; furthermore, although they are employing a great many energy weapons, you will have noticed that the majority of those weapons are high-efficiency, low-yield devices, thereby conserving resources. Their shields, too, appear to be carefully tuned and highly efficient— more efficient than our own, I would say."

"And?"

"And I would estimate, Captain, that they can maintain this level of conflict for another thirty years."

Janeway blinked, startled, and turned to face Tuvok.

"Thirty *years?*"

"Yes."

"That's not possible," Janeway said. "Space battles last minutes, or hours, not *years!*"

"Based on my own experience prior to encountering this phenomenon ahead of us, Captain, I would say that your generalization is sound," Tuvok agreed. "However, after studying the levels of damage being inflicted, analyzing the debris in the area and the contents of the dust cloud surrounding us, and measuring the background radiation, I am forced to conclude that the fleet action ahead of us has *already* lasted between six and eight hundred standard years."

"Six and eight *hundred . . . ?*"

Janeway stared at him. "How can they keep a battle going for centuries?"

"The capital ships appear to be fully self-contained, Captain," Tuvok said. "In theory, they could fight on indefinitely."

"But what kind of people could *do* that?" Janeway demanded, looking at Neelix.

The Talaxian held out his hands in a gesture of helplessness. "The Hachai and the P'nir do have some undeniably odd behaviors," he said.

CHAPTER
9

NEELIX WAS NOT CERTAIN, AT FIRST, WHETHER THE captain was speaking literally when she said to tell her all about the Hachai and the P'nir and their ancient, interminable war. He glanced uneasily about the bridge, and saw that everyone who was not actively involved with the controls or instruments was staring at him—Tuvok on one side, Harry Kim on the other, and Chakotay and the captain right there in the middle.

They did look as if they wanted him to tell them about it. He cleared his throat.

"Well, as I said before," he began, "the Hachai and the P'nir were always very good at defensive technology. They made the best shields in the quadrant, very highly tuned, very efficient equipment. They were both great believers in the value of defense."

Neelix paused and looked around, to see whether he should continue.

"Go on," Janeway told him.

"Well, as I heard it," Neelix said, "long ago, when the war began in earnest, both sides built defenses, and skimped on offensive weapons, and they insisted on staying with that sort of arrangement, despite what some of my . . . despite the attempts of certain parties to sell the Hachai some very good offensive weaponry at real *bargain* prices, prices that they were foolish to turn down . . ."

"Mr. Neelix," Janeway said warningly. The Talaxian stopped, startled, and looked at her.

"I assume these parties who dealt with the Hachai included Talaxians?" Janeway asked.

"Well, they might have," Neelix admitted.

"Never mind the comments on Hachai foolishness," Janeway said. "Get on with the story."

"Of course, Captain," Neelix said. He cleared his throat, brushed both hands down the front of his rather gaudy jacket, and continued.

"As I was saying," Neelix said, "both sides emphasized defense over offense, and the result was a stalemate. As I heard the story, both sides eventually came up with the same intended solution to the stalemate. Each side built a fleet of immense warships that were meant to sweep through the cluster, destroying anything that opposed them, and exterminating the enemy, planet by planet. These warships were entirely self-contained, with no need to return to base between attacks, so as to avoid any chance of their enemies ambushing supply runs, and so they could take as long as they needed to batter down planetary defenses."

Janeway nodded. "Go on," she said.

"The thing is," Neelix continued, "that both sides made the same mistake with the fleets that they'd made all along—they built them to be almost indestructible at the expense of the offensive weaponry. The two fleets destroyed a lot of worlds, you saw some of that, but when they finally met and started shooting at each other, well . . . nothing much happened, at least at first."

Neelix pointed past the forward console at the viewscreen. "When the fleets met, that battle out there started—and it's still going. Any new ship that either side built was sent to join the battle, because if it weren't, then the other side might win and their fleet would be free to sweep through the cluster. For centuries, the entire industrial production of the Kuriyar Cluster was devoted to pouring more and more ships into that battle, which pretty thoroughly ruined any trade prospects around here, and . . ."

Neelix caught the hardening of Janeway's expression and decided against explaining how much money this turn of events in the war had cost honest Talaxian arms dealers.

"Well, as you can see, Captain," he concluded, "the P'nir and the Hachai have both staked the future of their civilizations on it. The loser will doubtlessly be so weakened that the winner—if there ever *is* one—will be able to wipe the loser out completely. You saw that one planet back there, with the half-finished ship—it's defenseless. They're probably all like that."

"You said, 'If there is one'?" Janeway said.

"Your officer says the two fleets are evenly matched," Neelix said with a shrug. "Maybe they'll destroy each other completely."

"Their own version of Ragnarok," Tuvok remarked, stepping out from behind the sleek gray console.

Neelix blinked, and turned to look at the Vulcan. "Their own version of what?" he said.

"Ragnarok," Tuvok repeated, stepping down to the central level. "An old Earth myth, from the Norse cultures of the northwestern portion of the Eurasian continent."

"I'm not familiar with it," Neelix said.

Tuvok explained, "The Norse poets claimed that Odin, king of the group of gods known as the Aesir, had traded one of his eyes for knowledge of the future, and that knowledge included the details of the final battle between the Aesir and their bitter enemies, the Frost Giants. In this battle, which they called Ragnarok, both the gods and the Frost Giants would be utterly destroyed, and the world itself would perish with them. Although after Odin's bargain both sides now knew that this battle would mean their destruction, they were powerless to prevent its occurrence or to alter its outcome."

Neelix stared at the Vulcan. "What a depressing myth!" he said.

"It *is* depressing," Janeway agreed. "The ancient Norse were not a cheerful people."

"I think it's fascinating," Kes said.

"A more widespread Earth myth of a final battle is the prophecy of Armageddon," Tuvok said, "but in that tale it is confidently predicted that the forces of good will survive and triumph over the forces of evil. That seems less appropriate to the case here before us than the essential despair of the Ragnarok myth."

"Is there anything we can do about it?" Janeway asked. "I'm not eager to stand by and watch as two cultures destroy themselves." She looked down at the smear where the Hachai doll had been, then up at the viewscreen just as two of the alien warships collided and exploded spectacularly.

"One Hachai, one P'nir," Tuvok remarked. "The balance is maintained."

"Which is which?" Janeway asked.

"I do not know," Tuvok replied, turning to look at the screen. "I am able to readily differentiate the two sides by the design of their ships, but I have no way of determining with any certainty which are the P'nir and which the Hachai."

"The longer, thinner ships are the P'nir," Neelix said helpfully. "The dark ones."

"Thank you," Janeway said, as she studied the image on the screen.

Once she had that bit of information, and added

it to the memory of the unfinished Hachai ship they had seen on the ground, distinguishing the combatants was easy, despite the haze of debris and the blaze of weapons and energy fields.

The Hachai ships were smooth, bloated, rounded things, leaden gray, some of them painted with broad stripes of bright colors—orange and greenish-yellow, mostly.

The P'nir vessels were dark, jagged masses bristling with protrusions—antennae, gun turrets, and other, less-recognizable features. Where the P'nir showed any color at all, it was either sections painted in deep green or an occasional sigil in rich blood-red.

The unfinished starship on the primitive planet had indeed been a Hachai warship, she realized. Neelix had been right about that.

And the planet had not, she also saw, been preindustrial at all; it had been *post*industrial. They had put everything they had, every scrap of metal, into building their share of the immense fleet ahead.

The *entire cluster* had done that. All the metal, all the technology, everything worthwhile from two great civilizations was out there ahead of her, wrapped up in an immense orgy of destruction.

She wondered whether there had ever been any other intelligent species in the Kuriyar Cluster. If so, they must surely have been caught in the cross fire and destroyed long ago. . . .

Or had they? She glimpsed something in the

mass ahead that looked different. "Is there anything in there other than the Hachai and the P'nir?" she asked.

"Wreckage," Tuvok replied immediately.

"Anything else?"

Tuvok stepped back up and swung into his station, where studied his instruments; on the opposite side of the bridge Ensign Kim, too, initiated new, more detailed sensor sweeps.

"It would seem that there is, in fact, an object present that does not appear to be of Hachai or P'nir manufacture, or of natural origin," Tuvok said a moment later.

"Show me," Janeway said.

A blurry image appeared on the main viewer; Janeway knew that it was pieced together from a hundred quick glimpses and then enhanced by the ship's computers. A blue scale appeared beside it, to indicate its size, as well as outlines of a Hachai dreadnought and a P'nir battleship for comparison. To one side of the screen the computer provided a readout of the thing's emanations.

The object appeared to be roughly spherical and about two kilometers in diameter, most of its surface made up of hundreds of identical rounded cells, or facets, reminiscent of the cells in a honeycomb. This pattern was interrupted by several large, dark, irregular openings in the object's surface.

Janeway thought something about it looked almost familiar, but she couldn't place it.

"What *is* that, Mr. Tuvok?" Janeway asked. "A ship? A station?"

"I lack sufficient data to even guess, Captain," the Vulcan replied.

"Where is it in the battle?"

Tuvok tapped a few controls, and a schematic appeared on the viewer; the mysterious globe was near the center of the raging conflict between the P'nir and the Hachai.

"From the object's location, and the flow of the battle," Tuvok said, "it might even be what the two fleets are fighting over."

Janeway said, "Neelix?"

"I don't know, Captain," the alien replied. "No one outside the Kuriyar Cluster really knows what started the war. We mostly just thought of it as a personality conflict."

"Do you have any idea what that . . . that thing in there might be?"

"None at all, Captain."

"It's producing an interesting assortment of radiation," Chakotay remarked, as he studied readouts at the forward console, one hand tapping illuminated blue and gold keys. "Including some sorts I've never seen before—and Captain, including secondary tetryon radiation."

"Mr. Kim, could that be where the tetryon beam came from?" Janeway asked, turning to look up at Ops.

Kim hesitated, then said, "It's exactly on the line we traced back from the tetryon scan, Captain—

but that might just be a coincidence. And the secondary radiation *might* just be from the scan itself, if there's something in that thing's hull that reacts to tetryon bombardment."

"Or it might be internal resonance. Can you tell me anything more about the object?"

"I'm afraid not, Captain—with the battle around it, all the debris and those shields and interference from the weapons, we can't get any decent sensor readings from here. We'd need to be much closer, right inside the battle zone, to get a good look at it."

Janeway stared at the screen, considering.

That mysterious object was tempting—it might be their way home. It didn't look anything like the Array, but it still might be home to the Caretaker's companion.

And the carnage, the waste of this immense battle that was going on all around it was appalling. Two advanced civilizations were destroying themselves.

She remembered the three pitiful little mummies they had found in the asteroid tunnel. Those *people* were destroying themselves.

They had to be stopped.

The *Voyager* was hardly equipped to interfere directly, even if doing so weren't a violation of the Prime Directive, but surely, the P'nir and the Hachai must realize how wasteful and destructive this war was! Neelix had said that outsiders had avoided this area for centuries—except, perhaps, for arms traders, who would hardly be interested in peacemaking. The battle was drawing near a close, still undecided—thirty years to go, after more than six centuries of ferocious combat.

Maybe the P'nir and the Hachai would be ready to listen to reason.

Those children in that asteroid—surely, their relatives would listen to reason!

The Federation prided itself on providing arbitrators and negotiators for anyone who needed them. Janeway had never been trained for that sort of work—at least, no more than any starship captain had to be—but she could hardly make the situation any worse when both sides were already actively pursuing genocide. In another thirty years, if no one intervened, this entire cluster might be lifeless—or it might be ruled by a single species with a ruined economy and no assets except a massive interstellar war fleet, and wouldn't *that* be wonderful for the peace and security of the Delta Quadrant. The eventual victor would probably come sweeping out of the Kuriyar Cluster looking for worlds to conquer not out of any vicious need to dominate, but just so they could rebuild their own ruined cultures.

The Kazon-Ogla or some other local power might well prove to be a match for the P'nir or the Hachai, whichever the winner might turn out to be, but still, the rampage and eventual destruction of such a fleet was hardly anything to look forward to. If she were to just change course and travel on past, without at least *trying* to end this obscene slaughter, Janeway knew that she would be unable to live with herself—and all that was quite aside from the more personally important question of the tetryon beam's origin, or the nature of that strange spheroid. Had the scanning beam come from that globe? Was the Caretaker's companion in there?

Janeway had to at least attempt to intervene, to stop the slaughter and to get in there for a look at the globe—but what could she hope to do, with a single, relatively tiny ship?

All she could offer would be words. And before she started talking, it would help if she knew what to say, and knew whether any of these people were even slightly interested in listening to her.

Neither side had signaled the *Voyager,* or made any threatening moves toward the new arrival. What did that say about their intentions?

"Ensign Kim," she said, "is there any evidence that either the Hachai or the P'nir have detected our presence here?"

Kim hesitated. "I don't see how they could miss us, Captain; we aren't doing anything to hide, after all, and we're well within sensor range."

"They may be too busy with more immediate concerns just now," Janeway said dryly. "I know they *could* have seen us, but *have* they?"

"I don't know, Captain."

"No one's scanned us, or attempted to contact us?" Janeway asked.

"Not since the tetryon scan."

Janeway nodded. That was as she had expected. The Hachai and the P'nir were totally focused on each other. All the rest of the universe had ceased to exist, as far as they were concerned.

She would just have to remind them that there were other people out here.

"Hail them," she said.

Ensign Kim hesitated. "Hail *who?*" he asked. "There are thousands of ships out there!"

"Hail *all* of them, Mr. Kim," Janeway replied. "Hail them all, and let's see who answers."

Harry Kim turned unhappily to his controls.

"Hailing frequencies open," he said.

CHAPTER
10

"THIS IS CAPTAIN KATHRYN JANEWAY OF THE FEDERA-
tion starship *Voyager*," Janeway said, speaking
loudly and clearly. "May we offer our services as a
neutral party willing to help you negotiate your
disagreements?"

Her message sent, she sat down and waited for a
response—any response.

She didn't really expect the combatants to trust
her, or to take her up on her offer immediately, but
she did hope to stir up some sort of a reaction. If
this message didn't work, then she would try something else. She was not willing to just fly on past,
continuing on the *Voyager*'s long, long journey
home and leaving this insane war to drag on to its

sorry conclusion—and also leaving that unidentified object trapped in the midst of the combatants, leaving the origins of the tetryon beam a mystery. She knew that she might eventually have to do just that, to go on past; she knew that she might not be able to get the combatants to listen to her.

But to live with herself, she had to give it every possible effort first, and she knew that if she eventually did give up and move on, she would spend the rest of her life wondering if there were something more she might have tried.

"No reply, Captain," Harry Kim said.

She sighed. "Direct a hail to the nearest ship, then, on a tight beam—I don't care which side."

"There's a P'nir heavy cruiser that's moving along . . ." Kim began.

Janeway cut him off before he could finish his sentence. "That will do fine," she said.

"Hailing . . ." He waited, bent over his console, listening, then shook his head. "I'm sorry, Captain, they're refusing contact."

"Try a Hachai ship, then," Janeway ordered.

"Aye-aye," Kim said, tapping his controls. "Hailing."

Before Janeway could say anything more, the viewscreen lit up with the image of the Hachai bridge.

The design was unfamiliar, but intelligible; one Hachai, presumably the ship's commander, sat in a transparent globe at the center of an open space, surrounded by other Hachai perched at individual stations on at least three different levels—there might well have been additional areas not shown in the transmission.

The Hachai were fat bluish-gray creatures with stalked eyes and four multijointed arms apiece, just like the doll—or like the mummies. Janeway remembered that the mummies' legs had been hidden by rubble, and the doll's legs had been stubby little things that were pushed up into the toy's rounded bottom; she realized that she couldn't see any legs here, either. The Hachai presumably had legs, since the doll had had them, but Janeway couldn't see any. Perhaps they were retractable.

It was oddly pleasant, and oddly surprising, to see these living, breathing Hachai. It helped to lighten the memory of those sad little mummies.

"Your transmissions are not wanted," the Hachai commander said brusquely. "We will not listen to any of your P'nir trickery."

"There's no trickery," Janeway replied quickly. "We are merely a neutral party who does not wish to see anyone die unnecessarily. . . ."

The Hachai commander interrupted her.

"We must assume your presence is a P'nir trick of some sort," the Hachai said. "Perhaps it is intended to lure us into some folly, or merely to distract us. If you are not a P'nir deception, if you are truly a neutral party, then leave this area immediately—you are not welcome here."

"We are not . . ." Janeway began.

"If you do not leave," the Hachai captain said, cutting her off again, "we must assume that you are hostile, and we will respond accordingly. This is your final warning."

The screen went dark.

Janeway frowned. "Hail them again," she said.

"Hailing," Kim said. He shook his head. "They're refusing our hail."

Janeway considered their position. What else, she wondered, could they try?

Her thoughts were interrupted by a shout. "Captain!" Paris called. "The Hachai are breaking out of formation and coming toward us!"

"Onscreen!" Janeway said, leaning forward in her chair.

Sure enough, a single Hachai dreadnought had pulled free of the battle and was charging toward the *Voyager*. The bloated gray shape was expanding rapidly on the viewer.

"It's big," Chakotay said, unnecessarily; the Hachai ship that was bearing down on them was utterly gigantic, dwarfing the *Voyager*.

"Red alert," Janeway snapped. "Maximum shields. Hail them; ask what we can . . ."

"The Hachai ship is opening fire, Captain," Tuvok reported calmly. "It appears to be a multi-frequency phased energy beam. . . ."

The "phased energy beam" lit the viewer a vivid red for an instant; the screen flickered, and the bridge lights, already dimmed for the alert, dimmed even further briefly as the ship's power was diverted to the forward shields. The red light turned the gray carpet almost black, and the soft, colorful glow of the instrument panels stood out in sharp contrast.

Janeway watched as *Voyager*'s shields easily absorbed the Hachai's attack without transferring any of the destructive energy to the ship itself.

"She's veering away," Paris said. "Breaking off the attack."

"It was just a warning shot, then," Chakotay said.

"I would tend to agree with Commander Chakotay, Captain," Tuvok said. "The Hachai vessel fired at extreme range, then immediately turned aside."

"That weapon, Tuvok," Janeway asked, turning to her right, "what was it? What did you call it?"

"A phased energy beam," Tuvok replied from behind his console. "It was not a true phaser, but the product of a similar, somewhat more primitive technology."

Janeway considered that. Phasers had been the standard armament in the Federation for a century, and the technology had spread throughout the Alpha Quadrant—but apparently it wasn't so widespread here.

A phaser used a tuned monopolaric beam of coherent energy that could be modulated for various effects, from blocking nerve impulses without doing any other harm to the target all the way up to disrupting the strong nuclear force, which caused matter to disintegrate right down to the subatomic level.

Tuvok said the weapons in use here were something else, however.

"Give me the specs on that."

"On your screen, Captain," the Vulcan replied.

Janeway flipped up the panel by her chair and studied the display. As Tuvok had said, the weapons were not phasers; they projected coherent energy, but it wasn't monopolaric, which meant it could not be tuned properly. The phase could evidently be shifted up or down, which would alter its effects to some extent, but it would have nothing remotely like the versatility of the *Voyager*'s own weapons. These beams could not be set to stun, nor could they obliterate matter entirely; they could merely blast. That blast could be adjusted so that it was delivered as intense heat, or as a cutting beam, or in various other forms, but it was still far less effective than a phaser.

Apparently no one in the Kuriyar Cluster had ever developed the Kawamura-Franklin circuit that made true phasers possible.

"Is that the best they've got?" Janeway asked.

"I cannot say," Tuvok replied, "but it does appear to be their primary armament."

"Our shields handled it without any problem," Janeway commented.

"The shot was fired from extreme range," the Vulcan pointed out. "However, it would appear that our shields could, indeed, withstand a reasonably heavy assault by such weapons for quite some time."

"Years?" Janeway asked, looking up at the Vulcan, thinking of Tuvok's earlier estimate that the battle had thirty years left to run.

"No," Tuvok said. "The Hachai and P'nir shields would appear to be superior to our own in durability; in our present condition, the power consumption would drain *Voyager*'s engines relatively quickly, and our shields would then collapse. We could, however, survive at least a few hours of serious bombardment."

That was interesting; it opened up possibilities. It meant that if necessary, the *Voyager* could stay to talk to one side even while under attack by the other. That wasn't ordinarily any part of the role of a negotiator, but the situation here was not an ordinary one.

And there might be another possibility, as well, one bearing on their own needs.

"Could we survive long enough to reach that thing in there, that globe, and find out what it is?" she asked.

Tuvok hesitated.

"Could you rephrase the question, Captain?"

"I'm asking you, Mr. Tuvok," Janeway said, "what are our odds of reaching that object intact, if we go in there with our shields at full power and making whatever evasive maneuvers we can?"

"Captain, there are too many variables to give an exact answer. . . ."

"An approximation will do. What order of magnitude are we talking about here?"

"Our odds of survival would be several thousand to one against," Tuvok admitted, his expression slightly pained at having to give so imprecise a response.

"Why, if their weapons are so ineffective?" Chakotay demanded.

"It's not merely the phased-energy weapons we would need to worry about," Tuvok explained. "If you observe the battle, you will see that the participants are not significantly more vulnerable to such weapons than we are; the beams are used primarily to force the enemy in a chosen direction." He gestured at the screen. "What actual damage occurs is inflicted in several ways—by trapping a vessel in a sustained cross fire of a variety of weapons, thereby forcing shield overload and eventual failure; by crushing ships between the shield fields of several enemy ships; by forcing explosive devices or kinetic weapons through shields with pressor beams; but only rarely with the energy beams themselves. This is why the battle is so stable; it takes much careful maneuvering to trap a single enemy long enough to destroy it, and meanwhile the enemy is maneuvering to prevent that entrapment. . . ."

As he spoke, Janeway watched the main viewer and saw the Hachai dreadnought plunge back into the battle, taking a P'nir cruiser from one side and forcing it up against a smaller Hachai ship, while three other P'nir vessels moved into formation, enclosing the smaller Hachai—and on and on, the entire mass of ships all maneuvering around one another, trying to entrap and crush each other, just as Tuvok said.

"I see," Janeway said. "So you think we'd be trapped and destroyed somehow if we entered the battle zone?"

"Almost certainly. Unlike the Hachai and the P'nir, we have no allies who would come to our aid if either side chose to entrap us."

Janeway nodded.

"What if we *did* have allies?" Lieutenant Paris asked. "Suppose we sided with the P'nir? Couldn't we break the deadlock?"

"Why the P'nir?" Chakotay asked.

Paris swiveled to face the first officer. "Because the Hachai just *shot* at us, sir!" he replied.

"Just a warning shot," Chakotay said. "If they had really wanted to damage us they wouldn't have turned away after a single attack."

Janeway glanced up at Neelix, whose expression was almost desperate.

"I take it you'd choose to side with the Hachai, Neelix, if you had to choose?"

"If I had to choose, Captain," the Talaxian said, "yes, I'd pick the Hachai over the P'nir."

"So would I, I think," Janeway said, thinking of the huddled family in the tunnel and the little rag doll, "but then, I don't know anything about the P'nir; everything we've seen so far has been from the Hachai side."

"I don't think you'd like the P'nir as much, Captain," Neelix said. "But does it matter? You're not going in there."

Then he saw the expression on Janeway's face.

"You *aren't,* are you?" he asked, horrified.

CHAPTER

11

JANEWAY SIGHED. SHE WAS NOT PARTICULARLY EAGER to answer Neelix's question.

Reluctantly, she said, "No, we're not going to get ourselves openly involved in the battle. We're not going to help the Hachai against the P'nir, or the P'nir against the Hachai. Choosing sides in this conflict would be a clear violation of the Prime Directive."

"It would also probably get us all killed," Chakotay pointed out. "Even if we did manage to break the stalemate and give the victory to one side or the other, the chances that we'd survive doing it . . ."

He broke off, groping for words, then looked helplessly at Tuvok.

"Assuming that the side we choose to attack reacts in a logical manner by concentrating their forces against the new threat," the Vulcan said, "and further assuming that we attempt to withdraw at our best possible speed when unable to fight effectively, our chances of survival would be roughly three in one million."

Janeway glanced at her old friend. "Not one in a million?" she asked, smiling crookedly.

"No," Tuvok said. "Three in one million. Or approximately one in three hundred thirty-three thousand, if you prefer to state it that way."

"So much for tradition," Chakotay said.

"The logical thing for us to do," Tuvok said, "inasmuch as we are not equipped to intervene effectively, would be to detour around the battle entirely, and to proceed on toward the Alpha Quadrant."

"And ignore that tetryon beam?" Paris protested. "And that round . . . thing in there?"

"Precisely," Tuvok replied. "The evidence linking the spheroid to the tetryon beam is largely circumstantial and is inconclusive. Even adding in the additional time and energy required to make the detour, our odds of arriving home safely are measurably better if we do not involve ourselves in the conflict here."

"No," Janeway said, "We can't just go. That would leave the Hachai and the P'nir fighting each other until one side is wiped out."

"This is true," Tuvok answered. "The continuation of the battle to a final conclusion is unfortunate, but I see no way to prevent it."

"But we have to try," Janeway said. "We can't just walk away from mutual genocide. We have to *try* to stop it."

"You already *did* try," Neelix protested. "And they shot at you."

"We didn't try hard enough," Janeway insisted. "Neelix, all of you, don't you realize what will happen here when the battle finally ends? Whichever side it is that finally wins, when they've finished this fight they'll go home, and they'll find that their worlds are ruined—ruined or completely gone. They'll see that they've stripped themselves of all their resources, everything they ever had, to build these fleets. When the war is over, the victor will have nothing left *except* the fleet—whichever side it is will have to *use* that fleet, whatever's left of it, to survive."

Neelix's eyes widened.

"You mean . . ." He leaned on the railing and looked at the viewscreen. "I must admit, Captain, that the notion of a P'nir war fleet with nothing to stop it from rampaging across the galaxy is not a very happy one."

"Oh? Would a Hachai fleet be that much better?" Chakotay asked.

"Oh, yes," Neelix said, "unquestionably. You can bargain with the Hachai."

"Even when they've got you at gunpoint?" the first officer said.

"Well . . . that certainly does put one in a less advantageous position," Neelix admitted. "But really, the end of the war is still thirty years off, and what choice do we have? The captain *tried* to talk to them!"

"They didn't believe us," Janeway said. "We need to try again, some way they *will* believe—send an ambassador to each side, perhaps. . . ."

"We don't even know what they're fighting about," Paris said.

"That would be something the ambassadors would find out," Janeway said.

Chakotay looked at his captain. "You're determined to do this?" he said.

"Absolutely," Janeway replied immediately. "The Federation is dedicated to bringing peace; it's Starfleet's primary purpose."

Chakotay's expression did not reflect his thoughts, but he could not help remembering that his own recent encounters with Starfleet, prior to coming aboard the *Voyager,* had been anything but peaceful. He doubted any of the Maquis back in the Demilitarized Zone would say that the Federation was primarily dedicated to bringing peace—except perhaps when speaking with bitter irony.

He did not say that; he merely said, "We're a long, long way from the Federation, Captain." He resisted the temptation to add, "Even farther from the Federation than the Demilitarized Zone is."

"But we're still a part of Starfleet," Janeway said. "Peacemaking is still a part of our mission." She studied the display on the viewscreen, where the battle seethed with flaring energies. "Now, how . . ."

"I'll serve as one of your ambassadors," Chakotay said, interrupting her.

He had reached the decision very suddenly, and only in retrospect did he understand it himself. The Federation might not have managed to make a satisfactory peace in the Demilitarized Zone, and he might have his doubts about Starfleet's actual effectiveness in peacemaking, but peace was still a worthy ideal—the ideal of a just peace, anyway, not the peace of annihilation that seemed to be what the Hachai and the P'nir were headed for, or that the Cardassians intended for the Maquis.

Chakotay did not want to live with the knowledge, when he and the *Voyager* had left this place and continued on their long voyage home, that they were leaving behind any more devastated worlds like the ones that they had seen on their way here.

Surely, that ideal of peace was worth some effort, some risk.

Janeway clearly believed in Starfleet's dedication to that ideal, even if Chakotay didn't, and Chakotay believed in Janeway. Maybe out here, unencumbered by the Federation's historical and geopolitical baggage, Janeway and the *Voyager* could do some real good.

Janeway deserved a chance to do that.

And Chakotay also believed in himself. He couldn't think of anyone aboard the ship who might do a better job at peacemaking than he could. He had the real-world experience of war to make him appreciate peace.

And he had held that doll in his hands, imagining what it might have meant to its long-dead owner. He did not want any more Hachai to die needlessly.

And besides, that mysterious globe in there just might hold the key to sending them all home.

When he spoke Janeway turned, startled, to look at her first officer.

Chakotay would not have been her first choice. Before coming aboard the *Voyager* he had been commander of a Maquis ship, fighting an illegal war against the Cardassians, and doing a good job of it—hardly the first place one would look for a peacemaker.

But on the other hand, she had seen that he had a reverence for life, and an appreciation of peace, that he had learned from his Native American ancestors. She had seen his face when they looked at those blasted, ruined planets, and knew that he had suffered at the thought of what had taken place there, the thought of all the innocents who had died.

Chakotay had fought against the Cardassians, yes, but he had joined the Maquis because he had thought it necessary to defend his home, not out of some misguided quest for power or glory or adventure.

Still, even granting his good intentions, a love of peace did not in itself qualify him for the job.

"You aren't exactly a trained diplomat, Commander," she said.

"No," Chakotay agreed, "I'm a warrior." He nodded at the screen. "As are they. I think I will be able to understand these people as well as anyone aboard this ship could—except, perhaps, Neelix."

Janeway could hardly argue with that; she had great respect for Chakotay's abilities. And she could hardly send Neelix as her ambassador.

She considered a moment longer, then nodded.

"Good," she said. "Now, we can't use the transporter, not through all those shields out there; we'll need to use the shuttlecraft to deliver you."

"But we only have one functioning shuttlecraft," Paris protested. "I thought you wanted to send embassies to both sides."

"What I want, Mr. Paris, and what we can do, are not always the same thing," Janeway pointed out acerbically. "However, yes, I intend to send ambassadors to both sides. Unless Mr. Neelix would care to volunteer the use of *his* ship, our one shuttlecraft will have to deliver them both, that's all." She turned and looked up at the Talaxian.

"Oh, no," Neelix said, lifting both hands from the railing in a defensive gesture. "I'm not taking *my* ship any closer than this!"

Paris accepted this unenthusiastically.

"Chakotay has agreed to serve as one ambassador," Janeway said, swiveling to look at the Ops station. "I believe Ensign Bereyt has had some diplomatic experience back in the Bajoran system; Mr. Kim, would you please ask her to join the first officer in the shuttlebay? And we'll need a crew for the shuttle. . . ." Janeway began to turn back toward the helm, and toward Lieutenant Tom Paris—the best pilot aboard the *Voyager,* as everyone knew.

"I'll go," Harry Kim said.

Startled, Janeway turned back to the communications officer. "Oh?" she said.

"With the captain's permission, of course," Kim said hastily, his voice slightly unsteady. "You'll need Mr. Paris here, Captain, in case we stir up one side—I mean, if we approach the P'nir first, the Hachai might assume it's a trick and try to destroy the *Voyager.* . . ."

"Or vice versa," Chakotay said. "I agree, Captain—I'd be pleased if you would send Mr. Kim as my pilot, and keep Paris here on the *Voyager.*"

That statement startled Kim as much as Kim's volunteering had startled Janeway; he hadn't thought that Chakotay liked him much.

Of course, Kim immediately realized, it might just be that Chakotay liked Paris even less. Kim had not yet figured out the peculiar relationship between Paris and Chakotay—they seemed to despise one another, and yet to respect each other at the same time. Chakotay had considered Paris a mercenary and a traitor to the Maquis, while Paris, as far as Kim could see, seemed to think of Chakotay as an arrogant idealist, yet the two had saved each other's lives. . . .

But then, Kim thought, he wasn't very good at

figuring out people's motives, not even his own. He wasn't entirely sure why he'd volunteered to pilot the shuttlecraft, let alone what was going on behind Chakotay's forehead tattoo, or Paris's insouciant smile.

The captain looked Kim over thoughtfully; Kim wondered if she understood his motives better than he did. He rather thought she did.

"Very well," Janeway agreed. "And I think we'll want one more person aboard, as a backup, if for nothing else—Mr. Kim, have Mr. Rollins meet you at the shuttlebay."

"Yes, Captain!" Kim turned to his controls for a final moment, transmitting the order, before rising and heading for the turbolift.

Chakotay, moving with deliberate grace, followed Ensign Kim. He paused in the doorway long enough to say, "Wish us luck, Captain."

Before Janeway could respond, the lift door had closed and the two men were gone.

"Good luck," she said anyway, addressing the empty air of the bridge.

CHAPTER

12

"It's really quite beautiful," Kes said, staring at the main viewer.

Startled, Janeway turned to glance up at the Ocampa, wondering what she was looking at.

Kes, Janeway saw, was watching the same thing as most of the others on the bridge—the display on the main screen, showing the ongoing battle ahead of them.

"What's beautiful?" she asked.

"That," Kes said, pointing at the viewer.

"You mean the battle?" Janeway asked, puzzled. That seemed out of character for Kes. The Ocampa were not a warrior race, by any means; their underground civilization was peaceful, placid, and nonviolent. What beauty could one of them see in a genocidal war?

"Yes," Kes replied. She shifted her gaze from the screen to the captain and saw Janeway's expression. She glanced down at the smear of dark dust where the Hachai doll had lain, and then met Janeway's gaze again.

"I mean, it's beautiful if you don't know that it's thousands of sentient beings trying to kill each other," Kes tried to explain. "It's *visually* beautiful, at this distance, however horrible it may really be for the people involved. If you just look at the patterns, at the colors and shapes, then it *is,* it's beautiful."

Janeway turned to look at the screen, trying to see what Kes saw.

They were close enough to the battle now that even without magnification, it was no longer a distant ball of sparkling light; instead it was a sprawling amorphous mass where individual shapes could be made out, weaving about each other, cutting through the cloud of dust and debris left by their destroyed companions. Weapons flashed pink and gold and deep rich blue, energy beams appearing and disappearing, connecting one ship to another for an instant, then vanishing again as shields flared or the target dodged out of the line of fire. Formations arose, as if by spontaneous generation, to sweep through a particular sector or close in on a lone victim, only to break apart again into individual ships seconds later, when the enemy countered the move.

Janeway didn't see any patterns. The flickering colors of the weapons and the swooping trajectories of the ships looked random to her.

And she didn't see any beauty in that randomness; unlike Kes, she could not forget that those were ships out there, ships with living, breathing, sentient crews that were trying to kill one another by any means available. She could not forget the sight of those three pitiful Hachai mummies in the asteroid tunnel, killed when their entire world was destroyed by the P'nir; she could not forget that their relatives, three hundred years later, were still fighting and dying out there, and those deaths were what she and the rest of the people aboard the *Voyager* were watching.

There was no beauty in that.

Even if she tried to see it as something more abstract, as simply ships maneuvering rather than living beings killing one another, the bloated gray Hachai dreadnoughts and the spiky, shadowy P'nir cruisers did not fit any of her standards for what made a ship beautiful, either.

The battle seemed closer than it should be, too, she thought as she watched. Either the *Voyager* had been drifting, or some of the Hachai and P'nir ships had moved nearer to the *Voyager* in the course of their maneuvering about one another.

That made sense, she supposed; that Hachai warning shot had brought the one ship out this way, and the entire armadas would have shifted slightly to adjust for that. They *were* closer, no question about it, she realized—she could see more detail than ever.

Kes said she thought it was beautiful; Janeway stared, still unable to see any beauty in it.

As she watched, a Hachai shield buckled momentarily under heavy P'nir bombardment, and a burst of golden energy from one P'nir battery tore through the side of the ship; gas spouted forth, freezing instantly into a glittering white cloud as it dispersed into the vacuum of space. Three tiny tumbling shapes appeared, dark specks springing forth from the crystalline cloud—the corpses of Hachai crew members who had been sucked out through the ruptured hull.

The deflector shield was restored quickly— Janeway could imagine the near-panicky crew rushing to seal off the damaged sections, to reroute power and redirect the overlapping energy fields— and the Hachai ship sailed on, out of danger, its own weapons firing at two smaller P'nir vessels, its attacker swerving off in another direction.

The cloud of white crystals spread and dispersed, mingled with a band of dark metallic dust to create a swirling spiral of light and shadow. The three corpses were lost amid the drifting debris.

"Beautiful?" Janeway said, imagining those three corpses, their skin oils boiling away into vacuum, their internal fluids leaking out in spraying droplets as the bodies spun endlessly through space, three sentient lives destroyed, three people killed for nothing.

They would drift on forever, like the remains of

the P'nir orbital fortresses, or like the asteroidal remains of that shattered Hachai world. As their fluids evaporated into vacuum they would become three more freeze-dried Hachai mummies, until someday they might fall into a star, or burn up in a planet's atmosphere.

If some star traveler were to recover the bodies, centuries from now, they might well crumble to dust, as the Hachai doll had done.

And that all assumed, of course, that they weren't caught in the cross fire and reduced to their component atoms before they ever left the battle zone.

Janeway saw no beauty in any of that.

Kes looked at the glittering dust, the colored lights flaring and spattering through the vast flock of great ships as they swirled about one another, the constant interplay of shape and movement. "Yes," she said. "It's beautiful."

"I must agree, Captain," Tuvok said, looking up from his console. "The maneuvering of the two fleets is magnificently intricate, the equations describing their interactions quite elegant. The beauty of such things is undeniable."

Janeway suppressed a shudder. Much as she liked and admired her security chief, the dispassionate Vulcan attitude could still be unsettling at times.

"Janeway to Chakotay," she said, to distract herself, "are you prepared to launch?"

"Yes, Captain," came the first officer's reply. "Whenever you're ready."

Janeway signaled to Paris.

"Captain, it's not too late for me to go," Paris said. "Harry Kim doesn't belong . . ."

"Mr. Paris," Janeway snapped, "I want the shuttlebay doors open and the shuttle cleared for launch. I do *not* want an argument!"

"Yes, Captain," Paris replied quietly, turning his attention back to his controls. "Shuttle is cleared for launch," he announced.

A moment later Chakotay's voice came over the comm again.

"Shuttle away," he said. "I'll start broadcasting immediately, Captain, and then move in closer, away from the *Voyager.*"

"Not *too* close," Janeway answered. "We can't afford to lose the shuttle—or any of the four of you."

"Don't worry, Captain," Chakotay replied. "I've had experience at this sort of thing, remember—I know how close I can cut it."

Janeway bit back a response, resisting the temptation to remind Chakotay that at least once he'd misjudged, which was how he'd wound up aboard the *Voyager* instead of still commanding his own little ship in the Maquis guerrilla war against the Cardassians.

There was no point in nagging Chakotay. After all, he was no reckless daredevil to begin with— she glanced at Tom Paris as she thought that—and he had presumably learned from his experiences.

She watched the screen as the shuttle appeared, the familiar boxy outline silhouetted against the glare of the raging battle; she watched as the outline dwindled with distance, dwindled to little more than a shadowy dot on the flickering mass of light and color ahead.

Janeway didn't really have a good intuitive feel yet for the scale of the Hachai and P'nir ships, but it seemed to her that Chakotay was going a good bit closer than he really needed to; she quickly called up the shuttle's telemetry and confirmed her suspicion.

"Chakotay," she said, "back off; you're too near. A stray shot could hit you."

"My shields are at maximum, Captain," Chakotay replied calmly.

"You're in a *shuttlecraft,* Chakotay, not a starship," Janeway reminded him, "and those people out there are throwing around one hell of a lot of energy."

"I'll risk it, Captain."

Janeway hesitated.

Of course, she could order him not to risk it, to withdraw—but she had to trust her first officer's judgment. Even more than a starship captain always needed to be able to trust her officers, Janeway knew that to keep the peace aboard the *Voyager,* with her uneasy mix of Starfleet and Maquis crew members, she had to be *seen* to trust Chakotay. If that trust wasn't evident she might well undercut his authority with the Starfleet personnel, or build resentment among the Maquis.

If Chakotay thought he was safe enough where he was, she had to accept that.

"Just be careful," she said. "Run at the first sign of trouble. It's not our fight and we're outmatched."

"Understood, Captain," came the reply. "Now, let me make sure my broadcast is working. Chakotay out."

And then there was nothing for her to do but wait, Janeway thought, wait and see whether the Hachai or the P'nir would listen to the shuttle's broadcast offer to negotiate.

She turned and looked about the bridge, trying to find something to keep herself occupied while Chakotay was out there in his tiny little shuttlecraft, facing those thousands of warships.

Neelix, back by the turbolift, saw her looking about, and snatched the opportunity to address her.

"Captain Janeway," the Talaxian said, "couldn't we go somewhere else now? Somewhere farther from the battle? Perhaps we could come back when Commander Chakotay has had some time to talk . . ."

Janeway, concerned about her crew and annoyed at the little alien's endless attempts to get the *Voyager* away from the region, turned and said crisply, "Don't you have some cooking to do, Mr. Neelix?"

"You asked me to come to the bridge to advise you . . ." the Talaxian began.

"And you did," Janeway said. "Thank you. Now go away, please."

Neelix stared unhappily at her for a moment. He

thought of asking Janeway to at least allow him to take his own ship from the *Voyager's* shuttlebay and go somewhere else, somewhere safer—but she didn't look as if she was in any mood to be reasonable. He looked about, at Paris and Tuvok and the rest of the bridge crew; none of them looked particularly inclined to be reasonable, either.

He turned and headed for the turbolift. "Come, Kes," he said. "We know when we aren't wanted."

Kes hesitated, staring at the viewscreen, where a tiny dark shape hung before a seething mass of color and shadow. Then, reluctantly, she turned and followed.

CHAPTER

13

"THIS IS A FEDERATION SHUTTLECRAFT, OFFERING OUR services as a neutral party to aid in any negotiation or arbitration that the P'nir or Hachai might wish to undertake," the computer voice said. "Please contact us if you are willing to negotiate. This is a Federation shuttlecraft . . ."

Chakotay tapped a control and the speaker fell silent, leaving only the faint humming and hissing of the shuttle's life-support systems, but the four people aboard the shuttle all knew the message was still transmitting.

"They don't seem to be paying much attention, sir," Ensign Bereyt remarked.

"Give them time," Chakotay said. "Sometimes if you drum something into someone's head long enough, it will eventually penetrate." He settled back in his chair and looked around the interior of the little spacecraft.

Bereyt and Rollins were at the controls; Chakotay and Kim were off, for the moment. Harry Kim had gone back to see if there was any coffee on board.

That hadn't seemed very important to Chakotay when Kim suggested it, but thinking about it, he changed his mind. Coffee might be useful. The four of them might be sitting here aboard the shuttle for quite a while yet, he realized. They had come dashing out here without much of an actual plan— the plan was just "go out there and play ambassador," talk the Hachai and the P'nir into peace so that the crew of the *Voyager* could get a good close look at that mysterious globe.

But how could he play ambassador if the people he was supposed to talk to just ignored him?

Well, if they kept on playing that message, sooner or later someone might respond. If nothing else, someone might get sufficiently annoyed at its droning repetition to take a shot at them, and that might stir things up enough to get the other side talking.

Of course, that wouldn't do them much good if that first annoyed shot hit them. Chakotay looked at the control panels and frowned.

Could this shuttle hold up for more than a few seconds under any sort of attack?

"Ensign Bereyt," he said, "as long as we have some time to kill, why don't you and Rollins run a systems check on the shuttle? I don't think anyone's had the time to do one lately; B'Elanna Torres has been too busy keeping the *Voyager* intact to worry about this shuttlecraft, and Lieutenant Carey's been too busy watching Torres."

Chakotay noticed Rollins frowning; the barb at Carey had not been well received.

Well, it was too late to unsay the words.

"Yes, sir," Bereyt said. "I'll run a diagnostic immediately."

She didn't seem bothered, Chakotay noticed, either by his remark or by their present situation. Not all the Starfleet crew had bought into siding automatically with their own against the Maquis additions to the *Voyager's* crew, then.

Maybe, he mused, Bereyt, as a Bajoran, was a bit more sympathetic than most to the Maquis cause, or to any other fight against the Cardassians.

Or maybe she had just done a better job of leaving behind irrelevant old feuds; after all, the Maquis and the Cardassians and the Demilitarized Zone were all on the far side of the galaxy, and that nasty little war no longer had much of anything to do with getting the *Voyager* safely home—or with ending the Hachai-P'nir conflict.

The scale of the Hachai/P'nir war made the Maquis resistance look pretty trivial, really. Any one of those big ships out there could probably have polished off the entire Maquis resistance force in a matter of hours.

Or maybe he wasn't giving his own people enough credit; after all, the Cardassians had thought that *they* could wipe out the Maquis quickly, and at least up until the Caretaker yanked him across the galaxy, Chakotay hadn't seen it happening. The Maquis had been holding their own against the Cardassians—*and* against Starfleet.

He glanced over at the three Starfleet officers accompanying him.

Harry Kim was bringing four cups of coffee from the tiny galley in the stern; Bereyt and Rollins had started running the diagnostics.

Now they began calling out the results as Kim distributed the cups.

"Shields functioning normally and at full power, sir," Bereyt announced.

"Warp drive shows minor alignment problem, sir," Rollins reported an instant later. "It's harmless right now, but the matter-antimatter mix is less than optimal, and it'll get worse if we don't fix it."

Chakotay nodded an acknowledgment. "Go on with the checklist," he said.

"Life support fully operational," Bereyt said.

"Transporter fully operational," Rollins reported.

A moment later they had run through every system on board; everything checked out except the warp drive. "Ensign Rollins," Chakotay said, "see what you can do with that faulty alignment in the warp drive."

"Yes, sir." Rollins rose from his seat, heading for the access panel for the warp core. Harry Kim, standing to one side drinking his coffee, stepped out of the way.

It only took Rollins a few seconds to get the panel open and to start work. Chakotay watched as he reached in and began making the adjustments; he didn't seem very comfortable with the job.

But then, why should he? He was no engineer, he was a bridge officer.

Chakotay frowned, wondering if he should go lend Rollins a hand; after all, the Maquis hadn't had the luxury of excessive specialization. Every Maquis officer did a little of everything; Chakotay had tinkered with the engines once or twice, when B'Elanna Torres wasn't available.

Just then Harry Kim called out, "A P'nir ship coming this way, sir!"

Chakotay whirled and looked at the main viewscreen.

The battle loomed before them, filling their entire field of vision; the warships looped and twisted, maneuvering around each other in their intricate dance.

One of the jagged, bristling P'nir ships, however, had indeed come spinning out of that gigantic tangle, swooping toward the shuttlecraft.

Had someone gotten annoyed with them so quickly? Chakotay mentally traced its path back, and decided not.

"It's not after us," he said. "See? It was dodging that Hachai phalanx." He pointed to a hemispherical cluster of huge gray ships that was now dispersing, like the petals of a flower blooming.

"Oh," Kim said. He started to relax—then tensed again. "Sir . . . !" he said.

A Hachai dreadnought was breaking out of the melee in pursuit of the P'nir ship, and both were headed in the direction of the shuttlecraft.

The P'nir ship passed the shuttle, frighteningly close, but made no threatening move. The Hachai ship, in hot pursuit, was farther away, and not firing yet.

"I don't think . . ." Chakotay started to say; then he said, "Damn!"

Two more P'nir ships were coming out after the Hachai, and an entire wing of Hachai were responding.

"It's not really anything to do with *us,*" Chakotay said. "It's just the ordinary fluctuation and drift we've been seeing all along. Still, I don't think this location is going to be a very healthy one five minutes from now. Mr. Rollins, please turn us . . ."

He paused, as he realized Rollins wasn't seated at the controls.

Rollins was still working on the warp drive, his hands reaching in through the open access panel. Chakotay looked at the Starfleet ensign, and hoped he didn't see the man's hands trembling.

"Mr. Kim," Chakotay ordered, "go see if you can help Rollins with that."

"Aye-aye, Commander," Kim said, as he hurried aft.

"Ensign Bereyt, is our warp drive functional?" Chakotay asked.

"No, sir," Bereyt replied. "Ensign Rollins had to take it off line to make the adjustments."

"We have impulse power, though?"

"Yes, sir."

"Then get us out of here on impulse," Chakotay ordered. "Take us back to the *Voyager.*"

"Sir, I . . ." Bereyt stammered, then gestured helplessly at the viewer.

Chakotay's lips tightened as he understood what she was unable to put into words.

A firefight was going on out there, between the shuttle and the *Voyager;* the P'nir ship that had been first to break free of the main battle had hooked back across the shuttle's path, and the Hachai had turned to intercept, but had not followed it directly; instead the Hachai were spraying the intervening space with energy beams and, Chakotay realized, some sort of missiles—torpedoes of some kind, most likely.

Or mines; some of the missiles were slowing, then fading into near-invisibility. If the shuttle were to head back the way it had come, it might well run smack into one of those devices, whatever they were.

"Move us out laterally, Ensign," Chakotay said. "Get us clear however you can."

"Warp drive is back on line, sir," Rollins called from the stern.

"Wonderful," Chakotay muttered.

The spirits of space, like many of his people's more traditional spirits, sometimes showed a rather nasty sense of humor. The warp drive had been out of service for perhaps ninety seconds, at most;

naturally, those ninety seconds had been when it had been most needed.

To be honest, though, he wasn't sure he and Bereyt would have reacted in time to avoid entrapment even had they had full warp capability all along. The surge in the battle had happened *fast*.

"Sir, I . . . I can't find an opening anywhere," Bereyt said. "Every time I think I see one, another ship moves up to block it off."

Chakotay frowned. "Ensign Kim," he called, "are you as hot a pilot as your friend Paris?"

"No, sir," Kim replied instantly. "I'm not much of a pilot at all."

"Then I'll take the conn." Chakotay slid into one of the forward seats, switched control to his own panel, and studied the situation.

Bereyt was right; the two fleets had bubbled up and effectively surrounded the shuttle in a matter of seconds. They were no longer merely observers near the battle, watching from outside; they were *in* it.

They were four people in a lightly armed, lightly shielded shuttle, in the midst of several thousand gigantic and possibly hostile warships.

CHAPTER

14

"Captain," Tom Paris said, "look!"

The remark was completely unnecessary; Kathryn Janeway was already out of her seat and staring at the screen, watching as one of the almost-random surges in the battle engulfed the shuttle-craft.

One minute the shuttle had been safely outside the combat zone; the next, it was gone. A spurt of battling ships had sprayed up out of the main mass, like a solar flare rising, but instead of falling back it had drawn other ships out after it, as if the battle had grown an immense pseudopod.

And then the entire conflagration had shifted, and the battle's "surface" had re-formed—between the *Voyager* and the shuttlecraft.

Janeway stared at the screen, then turned to the Security/Tactical station.

"Tuvok," she said, "can they get safely out of there?"

"Insufficient data, Captain," Tuvok replied almost instantly. "We don't know whether the Hachai or the P'nir will target the shuttle, or whether both sides will continue to ignore it."

"Captain, we have to go in there and get them out!" Paris said.

"No," Janeway replied immediately, as she stared at the screen. "If the shuttlecraft can't escape the battle on its own, then the *Voyager* probably couldn't, either. I won't get all one hundred and forty of us killed for the sake of those four people."

"But, Captain," Paris protested, *"Voyager's* bigger and stronger and faster than the shuttle; our shields have five times the effectiveness! *At least* five times!"

Janeway frowned. Paris might have a valid point. Tuvok had said that the *Voyager's* shield could hold up to hours of Hachai or P'nir bombardment; he hadn't said anything about the shuttlecraft.

Tuvok would probably know what the shuttlecraft's shields *should* be capable of, but he wouldn't know their actual current status.

Well, there was one person on board who should know, whose job it was to know the state of all the ship's equipment.

"Janeway to Engineering," the captain said.

"Torres, how good are the shields on that shuttlecraft?"

In Engineering, B'Elanna Torres looked up from the warp core monitor panel, startled. Behind her the core itself shimmered a pale blue and throbbed with power.

"Shuttlecraft?" she asked. "What shuttlecraft? I've been too busy keeping *this* ship running properly to worry about the shuttlecraft!"

She glanced at a monitor, then turned and glowered at Lieutenant Carey, who happened to be passing by, padd in hand, on his way to check the neutron flux in the matter-antimatter mixture. "You, Carey," she snapped, "what sort of shape is our shuttlecraft in?"

"Excuse me?" Carey said, startled.

"The shuttlecraft!" Torres shouted. "The one the captain just asked about! What sort of shape is it in? When did anyone check it out?"

"We did the regular scheduled inspections," Carey said. "It's all in the log. . . ."

"Go away, then," Torres snapped, working the controls to call up the engineering logs.

She read quickly.

The *Voyager* had only one functioning shuttlecraft aboard at present, so there was no question of which one the captain meant; furthermore, the log included the shuttle's present crew roster, mission statement, and clearance for launch.

A glance at the present-status report told Torres where Chakotay, Kim, Rollins, and Bereyt were at the moment, which made it obvious why the captain was asking about the shuttlecraft's shields.

Torres bit her lip. She barely knew Rollins, didn't know Bereyt at all, but she and Chakotay had been through a lot together, and Harry Kim had been with her among the Ocampa, when the Caretaker had almost killed them both in its attempt to reproduce itself. What were the two of them doing, risking their necks out there?

She didn't have enough friends aboard the *Voyager* that she could afford to lose those two.

The current situation was right there in the status report, but she had to look a good bit farther back in the log to find the maintenance records she wanted. She read through them quickly.

There weren't any reported problems in any of the shuttlecraft's equipment, nothing was scheduled for repair—but the date stamp on the last entry made her nervous. She tapped her combadge.

"Engineering to bridge," she said. "Captain, no one's done a real systems check on that shuttle since before our little encounter with the Caretaker; it was due for inspection the day after tomorrow. Given the rough ride we all had getting here, and Starfleet's idea of proper maintenance these days . . ." She took a deep breath. "Captain, we need to go in there and get it out."

On the bridge Janeway heard this and shook her head quickly, one sharp little jerk, even though she knew Torres couldn't see it. "Impossible," she replied.

She could see Paris's shoulders tensing at Torres's seconding of his own opinion; the red shoulders of his uniform exaggerated the motion, made it stand out from the soothing gray of the bridge walls. She ignored that, and gave him his orders.

"Take us in closer, Mr. Paris, ready to tractor the shuttle away if it breaks clear," she said. "But we will *not* enter the battle zone ourselves. It's up to Commander Chakotay to get the shuttle out of there."

"Aren't you going to at least talk to them, find out if there's anything we can do?" Paris protested.

"No," Janeway said. "They know we're here, and they can call us if they need to. The fact that they haven't done so, Mr. Paris, I take to mean that they're too busy right now, and I'm not going to distract them."

"And you aren't going after them?"

"I believe I've already answered that, Mr. Paris," Janeway replied sharply.

"But look at that cross fire! They . . ." Paris caught himself. "Aye-aye," he said reluctantly.

He watched intently as the great warships spun and danced through the heavens, the tiny shuttle almost lost among them, like a mouse amid a herd of elephants, ignored but in constant danger of being stepped on.

He expected the shuttle to be caught in a cross fire at any second, to flare up as its shields overloaded and then explode into glittering dust. He watched closely as the shuttlecraft maneuvered, vanishing from sight behind one gigantic ship for a moment, then reappearing briefly before it was obscured by another.

Paris knew that if he were aboard that shuttle, at those controls, he could have gotten it out in one piece—he found himself anticipating the shuttle's every move, and thinking what he would have done instead, were he the pilot.

He watched Chakotay, or whoever was at the conn, dodging about, trying to keep clear of the swarming combatants. Whoever the pilot was, he was doing the right things, but not quite fast enough—he was missing opportunities. And he was being too conventional—if he'd do something totally unexpected, he might find an opening.

The shuttlecraft dodged madly as Paris watched. Port, port, starboard, down, port, up . . .

And then Tom Paris blinked in surprise. He'd been thinking that Chakotay had to do something totally unexpected, and Chakotay had just done so—but why had he done *that*?

"What the hell are you *doing?*" he said aloud.

CHAPTER

15

At the precise moment that Tom Paris asked his question from the helm of the *Voyager*, Ensign Rollins, aboard the shuttle, spoke those exact same words.

"What the hell are you *doing*, Commander?"

"Trying to save our lives," Chakotay said. "Mr. Kim, hail them."

Harry Kim didn't need to ask who he should hail; a few seconds before, realizing he was rapidly running out of room to maneuver, Chakotay had sent the shuttle diving straight toward a P'nir cruiser that was not, at the moment, directly involved in combat with anyone.

Obviously, Chakotay wanted Kim to hail the P'nir ship.

"We're going to hit their shields in about four seconds," Bereyt said, her tone oddly calm. "Our own shields will buckle on impact, and the feedback will wreck the ship, even if we survive the collision. Which we won't."

That statement used up the four seconds, but by the time Bereyt was midway through her second sentence Chakotay had abruptly veered off, preventing a collision but sending the shuttlecraft skimming over the surface of the P'nir ship's shields close enough to trigger vivid blue flickers of interference.

"Hailing frequencies open," Kim said, "but they're not responding."

"You aboard the P'nir vessel," Chakotay said loudly, "this is the Federation envoy, respectfully requesting permission to come aboard."

Kim's jaw dropped; Rollins turned to stare at the first officer.

"You want to *board,* sir?" Rollins asked.

Chakotay looked at the others. "That *is* what we came out here for, isn't it? To go aboard their ships and play ambassador? Well, we've come this far; we might as well give it a try."

Rollins turned back to the controls. "They're not responding," he said.

"This is the Federation envoy," Chakotay repeated. "Let us aboard!"

"They still . . ." Rollins began.

Just then the cruiser's main batteries fired, from the side where the shuttle had first approached—but where they no longer were.

"Were they trying for us?" Rollins asked.

"No," Chakotay said. "They were—"

"They've dropped their shields!" Kim shouted, interrupting him.

Then the shuttle jerked, hard.

"What was that?" Rollins asked.

"Tractor beam," Chakotay said calmly, as he shut down the shuttle's main drive and allowed the little ship to be hauled in toward the P'nir cruiser.

"Their shields are up again," Kim announced, "but we're *inside* them."

"Of course," Chakotay said. "They fired that salvo to fend off the Hachai long enough to get us inside."

Kim and Rollins stared at him; Bereyt kept her eyes on the viewscreens.

"That's why I chose to try the P'nir," Chakotay explained. "Neelix had described the Hachai as paranoid, but he said the P'nir could be whimsical; I knew we'd have no chance with the Hachai, but if we did something absurdly risky, there was a chance it might catch the P'nir captain's fancy, and he or she would decide to capture us, rather than simply blowing us to bits."

"And it worked," Kim said, admiringly. "So we're alive and safe."

"I wouldn't say *safe*," Chakotay replied. "His *next* whim might be to blow us to bits after all. They don't really seem to be interested in negotiating, so we don't really have much to offer them, do we?"

Kim turned to glance at the rapidly approaching

side of the P'nir cruiser. A hangar door had dilated directly before them, plainly their intended destination; the light inside was an unhealthy green.

"We may have more than they think, though," Chakotay said thoughtfully, as he studied the P'nir ship.

"Commander?" Rollins asked.

"We've already seen that with the possible exception of their shields their technology looks slightly less advanced than our own," Chakotay explained, "and we know that transporter technology isn't common in this quadrant. We may well have a few surprises for them." He turned. "Mr. Kim, grab an environmental suit and get to the transporter; Ensign Bereyt, drop the shields, and then scan that ship and find us some quiet, unoccupied nook where we can put Mr. Kim, in case we need a little backup."

"An environmental suit, sir?" Rollins asked, puzzled.

"We don't know yet what the P'nir breathe," Chakotay explained.

"Yes, sir," Rollins replied, feeling foolish.

Just then the shuttle landed with a bump in the P'nir hangar, jarring the four of them. Ensign Kim dropped the bundle he was holding.

"Their air is breathable, sir," Bereyt reported. "It won't smell good, but it's nontoxic and has plenty of oxygen."

"Forget the suit, then," Chakotay called.

"I've got the coordinates of what appears to be a storeroom four decks down," Bereyt said.

"Good." He turned to see that Kim was in position. "Energize."

Harry Kim flashed and vanished.

Almost the instant the last sparkle of the transporter effect had faded, while the hangar door was still spiraling shut and the hangar bay was still filling with the thick P'nir atmosphere, a strange, flat voice came from the shuttlecraft's speakers.

"Leave your vessel immediately," the voice said. "Emerge unarmed."

Rollins glanced at Chakotay. Chakotay demanded, "How many of us?"

No one answered, and Chakotay repeated, "Tell us how many of us must emerge unarmed!"

"All three of you," the voice replied.

The three officers looked at one another.

"Well, I guess we won't be sending Harry any company just yet," Chakotay remarked.

"You have eight seconds," the P'nir voice informed them. "Comply."

Chakotay sighed. "Come on," he said.

Together, the three of them emerged into the green-lit gloom of the P'nir hangar bay.

Aboard the *Voyager* Tom Paris stared at the sensor reports. "They've been taken aboard the P'nir cruiser," he reported, his tone disbelieving.

"At least they're still alive," Janeway answered, relieved. She had been pacing back and forth across the central level of the bridge, from Ops to Security and back; now she stopped somewhere near the center and said, "Open a channel to the P'nir ship, if you can."

"Hailing."

Janeway glanced about the bridge while waiting for a response. It seemed oddly empty with Chakotay, Kim, and Rollins gone; for a moment she even regretted chasing Neelix and Kes away. The soft hum of the engines seemed to emphasize how quiet it was, and the soothing grays seemed drab.

"Captain," Tuvok said, "look."

Janeway's gaze returned to the main viewscreen just in time to see a Hachai dreadnought swinging out of the melee and moving toward the *Voyager.*

It would appear that someone was finally going to pay attention to them.

"Red alert!" she called.

The lights dimmed, and the grays turned dark, almost ominous, as red warning lights came on. Paris seemingly paid no attention; the ship remained on station.

"Lieutenant," Janeway snapped.

Paris looked up, startled.

"They're hailing us, Captain," he said.

"Who is hailing us, Mr. Paris?" Janeway asked. "You mean the P'nir are responding?"

"No, sir—I mean, Captain. I mean the Hachai are hailing us." He nodded toward the dreadnought.

"Onscreen."

The image of the battle vanished, and a Hachai commander in his transparent bubble appeared.

"We warned you," the Hachai said, without preamble. "Still you send your devices to the P'nir, you attempt to speak to them. We cannot allow you to aid them further. If you remain within six hundred thousand kilometers of any Hachai vessel or installation, we will destroy you."

"Four of our people have been taken prisoner . . ." Janeway began.

"No P'nir tricks!" the Hachai shouted. "No more *thagn* tricks!"

Then the image vanished, and the exterior view reappeared. At the center of the screen the Hachai dreadnaught loomed ever closer, blocking out much of the battle.

A part of Janeway found the time to wonder just what the word *thagn* might mean, and why the Universal Translator was unable to render it into intelligibility; she supposed it was an obscenity unique to the Hachai. Some interesting possibilities were suggested by eyestalks and retractable legs. . . .

"They've ceased transmission," Paris said, unnecessarily. "And . . ."

He didn't need to complete the sentence; when the viewer flared Janeway could see for herself that the Hachai had opened fire.

Accurately, too; the first shot had struck the *Voyager* dead on.

"Shields holding," Tuvok reported. "Shall we return fire, Captain?"

"No," Janeway said. "It's not our fight, it's a misunderstanding. Take evasive action, Mr. Paris, but make no hostile moves."

"We're not leaving?" Paris asked.

"No," Janeway said. "Of course we aren't. Our people are still in there somewhere. That globe is in there, too. We aren't going anywhere; just dodge as much of their fire as you can."

"Aye-aye."

The ship lurched, and Janeway was unsure whether it was Paris's piloting or Hachai fire that was responsible. The image on the viewscreen zigzagged wildly for a moment.

"Captain," Paris said, "should I try to get closer to the P'nir ship that captured the shuttle?"

Janeway had to swiftly weigh several considerations against one another before she could answer that. The Hachai would see it as further proof that the *Voyager* was part of some P'nir conspiracy if they moved closer—but the Hachai had already made up their minds, and to move farther away from the cruiser would be to reduce the chances of ever retrieving the shuttle or its crew.

"Do it, Mr. Paris," she said. "Get as close as you safely can."

"Captain, I would advise against . . ." Tuvok began.

A Hachai barrage interrupted the Vulcan's objection; the bridge lights flickered as the shields drained power. The image on the main viewer was now a constant glare of color and light as Hachai weapons blazed, filling the screen.

"Our shields are still holding," Tuvok reported. "Captain, I would advise against moving the *Voyager* any closer. You will remember how the shuttlecraft was caught up in the battle when . . ."

"Yes, I remember," Janeway said. "We'll just have to risk it."

Then she realized that Tuvok, in an utterly atypical action, had stopped speaking in the middle of a sentence before she had interrupted him. She turned, startled, to see what had so disturbed him.

"I am afraid that *risk* is no longer the appropriate term," the Vulcan said.

"Why not?" Janeway asked, turning to look at the main viewer.

"Tactical onscreen," Tuvok said.

The heat and fury of the actual battle vanished from the big screen, to be instantly replaced by the cool precision of a three-dimensional schematic computer display representing the battle in diagram form.

A white outline represented the *Voyager;* red circles indicated the Hachai ships, and blue triangles stood for the P'nir. The red and blue shapes formed an irregular spheroid with fairly clear boundaries.

And the white outline of the *Voyager* was already well inside those bounds.

CHAPTER
16

HARRY KIM ARRIVED ABOARD THE P'NIR CRUISER IN utter darkness. The glow of the transporter field gave him an instant of vision before it vanished, and he glimpsed a tall, narrow chamber around him, one side of it stacked with dark, rounded shapes.

Then he was fully materialized, the transporter field was gone, and he saw only black.

For a moment he stood there, listening, getting a feel for his surroundings.

The air was heavy and foul-smelling; the gravity was light, at most no more than half of Earth standard, he judged. He could hear nothing but a very faint, steady hum that was probably the residual vibration of the ship's main drive, filtered through the decks and bulkheads. It was subtly different from the familiar hum aboard the *Voyager*.

Everything seemed very still. It was hard to believe he was in the middle of a battle.

Then something thudded somewhere, far off, and the deck seemed to shift very slightly beneath his feet—the P'nir ship had probably just been attacked. Down here, deep within the immense vessel, it hadn't felt like much, but there had probably been a staggering amount of energy released.

Unless that distant thud had been the shuttle-craft coming to rest in the hangar bay, four decks up and a few hundred meters over.

That thought reminded him that Commander Chakotay and the others might need his help, and that he couldn't just stand here in the dark forever.

Moving slowly, hands extended, he felt his way across the room to a wall; there he put his back to the wall and paused for a moment, thinking.

He hadn't brought a light. He *should* have brought one, he told himself—he should have thought of that.

If he'd brought the environmental suit he'd have had a light, since one was built into the helmet, but he'd dropped the suit back on the shuttle before stepping into the transporter, so as not to weigh himself down unnecessarily.

He had a fully charged phaser on his belt—it had been obvious that if he was going to be sneaking around a possibly hostile warship, he needed a weapon—but he hadn't thought of bringing a light.

Commander Chakotay hadn't said anything about it; perhaps he hadn't thought of it either, or he'd thought it was so obvious it didn't need to be mentioned.

That was a trick the instructors back at the Academy had been fond of—not mentioning some basic element of the problem at hand because, as they always explained later, it was so obvious that it went without saying.

Kim had always hated that particular stunt.

This wasn't the Academy, though, this was real life, this was an alien starship, and whatever Chakotay had or hadn't thought or said, *Harry* should have thought of it. A Starfleet officer was supposed to think of everything. That had been the *point* of all those exercises back at the Academy.

Well, he told himself, he *hadn't* thought of it, and now he just had to live with that, and he'd have to make do with what he had.

Making do had also been a frequent subject of lessons at the Academy.

The room presumably had lights somewhere, if he could find them and turn them on—or did it? Maybe the P'nir didn't use visible light to see. That greenish glow from the hangar bay might have been unintentional.

Most intelligent species used visible light, though; some were blind, some saw entirely in the infrared or ultraviolet, but most had vision in a range that overlapped with human eyesight.

So there was *probably* some way to illuminate this room, but Harry had no way of knowing how the switch worked, or where it was.

He could use his phaser to heat something until it glowed; that was a standard Starfleet emergency method for lighting caves, for example.

This wasn't a cave, though; those bundles he had glimpsed when he first materialized might well be full of something flammable. Firing his phaser in here could be dangerous. Even if it didn't set off an explosion or start a fire, it might show up on the ship's internal sensors and get a security team hunting for him.

He'd just have to do without light, then—at least for now. From the brief glimpse he'd had upon arrival, and the near-total silence, he was fairly certain that the room he was in had been unoccupied until he had appeared in it, so he was safe for the moment.

All he had to do was get out of here, get back to the hangar and find out what had happened to the others. . . .

At that thought he reached for his combadge, but caught himself before he touched it. His presence on board was supposed to be a secret; it would not do to give it away by calling Commander Chakotay while the first officer was surrounded by P'nir.

Light or no light, he would have to find his own way around for now.

Cautiously, he began feeling his way along the wall, searching for a door.

As Harry Kim groped in the darkness, Commander Chakotay stepped down from the shuttlecraft door and got his first good look at the P'nir—or as good a look as was possible in the low, oddly colored illumination of the hangar area.

He also got his first good whiff of their air. It stank, an oily, metallic stench reminiscent of a badly maintained machine shop. He ignored that, though, and studied the half-dozen beings facing him from a few meters away.

These were the dreaded P'nir.

At least, he assumed these were the P'nir, but they were so motionless he could almost have taken them for sculptures of some sort. And of course, they might have been a slave species, or allies of the P'nir, but for now, he decided to assume that they were the P'nir themselves.

They were tall, about three meters from the tops of their heads to the deck, with gleaming blue-black skin—or perhaps exoskeletons, rather than skin; the surfaces looked hard and brittle. In the sickly greenish light Chakotay could not be sure whether that appearance was accurate; he thought that once he saw these beings move he'd know for certain, but at the moment the six P'nir facing him were absolutely, inhumanly still.

They stood on two legs, with an upright trunk and a head—roughly humanoid. Each P'nir had four arms, however—two on each side of its body, right up at the shoulder—which was rare among humanoids. That, combined with the chitinous flesh, gave them a vaguely insectile look.

The faces weren't insectile, though; they looked more like blank oval masks. Two pairs of red eyes gleamed from horizontal slits, looking nothing at all like the faceted eyes of insects. Each face had a serrated lower edge that might have indicated a mouth or nostrils; presumably these creatures breathed somehow, but whatever openings they used for that purpose were not visible.

There were no facial features other than the eyes and that serrated edge. If the creatures had external ears or other sense organs, Chakotay didn't see them.

He did see the weapons in their complex claws, though, and he held out his own empty hands in a gesture of peace—or surrender.

"Go to your left," a P'nir said—with no mouths visible, Chakotay was not entirely sure which one spoke.

"We wish to speak to your captain," Chakotay replied, speaking loudly and clearly.

"Go to your left," the P'nir repeated, and now Chakotay was sure that it was the one second from the left that had spoken, as it made an emphatic gesture with one of its right arms.

The arms bent at two elbows apiece, and the sections between joints remained completely rigid—those *were* exoskeletons, then, Chakotay was sure. It was very unusual for creatures as large as these to have exoskeletons; the cube-square law usually made it impractical. The P'nir must have evolved in a low-gravity environment.

The gravity aboard their ship did seem rather

light, in fact; Chakotay lifted a foot experimentally. Yes, it came up very easily.

"Is that the way to meet your captain?" Rollins asked from behind Chakotay.

"Go!" the P'nir ordered, flexing three arms angrily and pointing its weapon at the humans with the fourth.

"I think we should go," Chakotay said, turning left and ambling along at a speed much slower than necessary, even in the lighter gravity—and it *was* lighter, definitely; Chakotay estimated it at perhaps one-third of Earth's, similar to what he had lived with during his long-ago visits to Mars.

He had had enough experience working in low-gravity environments that if he had wanted to, he could have bounded along like a kangaroo—the passages, intended for the much-taller P'nir, provided plenty of room for leaping.

He did not leap; instead, he kept his steps low and slow, and Rollins and Bereyt followed his lead.

The languid pace was not intended to deliberately anger their captors; the P'nir were probably not sufficiently familiar with the movements of soft-skinned sentients to recognize a slow, easy stroll. Rather, Chakotay wanted time to observe, to think, and to plan before they arrived wherever the P'nir were directing them.

Besides, there was no point in tensing up, not until they knew more of their situation.

Behind him, Ensign Bereyt closed the shuttle-craft door before following. That wouldn't keep out the P'nir if they were determined to get inside but it might deter casual looting—and it would make it that much harder for the P'nir to discover the transporter and figure out what it did.

It was a shame that transporters didn't work through shields, Chakotay thought, or they could all simply have transported back to the *Voyager,* rather than allowing themselves to be captured.

And they *were* captured; while manners varied drastically from one species to the next, the P'nir were plainly not treating them as guests. Their P'nir escorts were armed, while they were not, and they had been ordered to leave the shuttle and go where they were directed, not invited.

Chakotay walked from the hangar area into a high, narrow corridor, and proceeded slowly onward. The corridor smelled just as bad as the hangar, and was lit with the same dull greenish light; the walls were black, with occasional incomprehensible markings on them in red or dark green, always well above eye level. That brought back odd memories of childhood, when Chakotay had so often been surrounded by things made for adults, things far too big for him.

Nothing back home had been proportioned like this, though, nor had he ever before encountered such an unpleasant color scheme. He walked slowly, and refused to look up at the designs on the walls.

The P'nir weren't hurrying them, at any rate; probably they didn't realize that humans could move faster than this.

"Go to the right," a P'nir ordered from somewhere behind them.

At the next opportunity Chakotay turned right, through an open door into a chamber.

It didn't look much like a conference room where an envoy might meet with the ship's captain; the only furnishings were several horizontal bars projecting from two of the walls, above the height of his own head. The bars seemed to be in pairs, one above another but slightly offset. He glanced from the bars to the P'nir, and guessed that those were at the right height for them to lean their four arms on.

For humans—or Bajorans—the bars wouldn't be much use at all. He supposed they could swing from them if they wanted to practice their gymnastics.

The chamber walls were black, unrelieved by any of the red or green—hardly cheerful in appearance.

"Tell me, are we to meet your captain here?" Chakotay asked as Rollins and Bereyt stepped into the room.

"No," the nearest P'nir said. It did not enter the room; instead it pressed a control, and a forcefield flashed into being, filling the doorway with a pale blue glow and sealing the three prisoners in.

Then the P'nir turned and marched away, leaving the three of them sealed in the black-walled, unfurnished chamber.

"What a surprise," Rollins said bitterly. "So much for diplomacy."

"Maybe," Chakotay said. "Maybe not. They haven't killed us yet."

Rollins cocked his head to one side and peered sideways at Chakotay.

"Not yet," he agreed.

"If they were going to, if that was all they planned, they would have done it," Chakotay said.

"Not necessarily, sir," Bereyt pointed out. "They might want to make a public example of us—the Cardassians did that sometimes. Or perhaps some officer wants the pleasure of torturing us to death for his own amusement; a few of the Cardassians did *that,* too."

"So I've heard," Chakotay admitted, wishing that Bereyt had kept her mouth shut. This sort of speculation was not going to be good for the morale of the others.

He wondered whether Bereyt really knew what she was talking about. For himself, he didn't know firsthand of any such Cardassian behavior.

But then, his own war against the Cardassians had been relatively brief, and largely fought openly, in ship-to-ship combat or air-to-ground raids; he had not lived with the grinding, endless terror of the Cardassian occupation the way the Bajorans had.

He had heard the stories, though. The Maquis had delighted in recounting Cardassian atrocities to one another, to help them work up the necessary hatred to maintain their fighting spirit. Some of the stories had doubtless grown in the telling, as all tales tend to do, but Chakotay had no doubt that there had been a few genuine sadists among the Cardassians who had used the occupation to indulge their perverted tastes.

But it had been only a few, and those had been Cardassians, not P'nir.

"I don't think it's very likely that this species goes in for torture," he said. "I would guess that those exoskeletons would make it difficult to inflict painful injuries without doing very serious damage. The . . . *art* would never have been developed."

"You never know," Rollins said. "They might have learned on other species."

Chakotay studied the ensign for a moment before replying, "Aren't *we* the cheerful bunch. All right, so we don't know what to expect from the P'nir; that's no reason for us to assume the worst. Yes, we're prisoners, but they may be negotiating with Captain Janeway for our release right now. As long as we're alive, there's hope. And don't forget Ensign Kim; he's out there somewhere."

"Yes, sir," Rollins replied wearily. "I haven't forgotten Harry Kim."

CHAPTER
17

THE SHIP SHUDDERED; JANEWAY GRABBED AT A RAIL-
ing to steady herself.

"Engineering!" she shouted. "Can you give us
additional power for the shields?"

Engineering was a madhouse; crew members
were hurrying about, trying to steady the energy
flows that kept the ship running despite the fluctu-
ating feedback from the battered shields. The feedback was plainly perceptible here as deep thudding
whenever the Hachai attacked, and an uneven
vibration in the deckplates beneath their feet. The
steady blue-white glow of the warp core seemed to
have intensified, but that was only because the
regular lighting had dimmed as power was diverted
to the defensive systems.

In the midst of chaos the chief engineer leaned forward to shout into the communicator.

"Sorry, Captain," B'Elanna Torres replied, as she struggled to do a dozen things simultaneously, "you've got whatever power we can spare." Then she noticed a readout. "But I'll try," she said.

She worked the controls, then smiled.

"You've got it," she said.

Sometimes, Torres thought, the *Voyager*'s state-of-the-art bioneural computer net could be a real nuisance; like most new, relatively untried technology, it was finicky and prone to unforeseen problems.

Sometimes, though, it worked just the way it was supposed to, and when that happened the bioneural equipment was an unmitigated delight.

That was the case now; the computer had been suffering from excessive heat leaking through from the raging battle outside, and had, acting entirely on its own in the interest of self-preservation, begun using the ship's recycling systems to convert waste heat to usable energy. It had been directing this energy to reserve, but the tap of a button let Torres redirect it to the shields.

Torres enjoyed having decent equipment to work with; in her years with the Maquis all she'd had was outmoded junk. Now, if she only had a source for spare parts, she thought, life would be just about perfect—at least, the portion of her life that centered on her work.

And that assumed, of course, that her life wasn't about to come to an abrupt end.

The ship shook suddenly, and the energy reading for the shields dipped slightly. Somewhere something hissed sharply as a conduit buckled.

"What the hell is going on out there, anyway?" she asked a nearby crewman—she didn't remember his name; many of these Starfleet people in their tidy uniforms still looked pretty much alike to her, and this wasn't one of the regular Engineering personnel, just someone running an errand. "Who are those people, and what are they fighting about?"

"I don't know, Lieutenant," the man replied, "but it's one hell of a big battle out there. Mr. Tuvok compared it to Ragnarok."

Torres stared at him. "What's Ragnarok?"

The crewman blinked. "The final battle of the Norse gods," he said. "You know."

"I do?" Torres asked.

"Uh . . . you didn't know?" He blinked again, and belatedly added, "Sir?"

"No," Torres said. "I know who the Norse gods were—Thor and Odin, right? Or were those Greek? But I never heard of this Ragnarok thing—why would I?"

"Well, I thought—I mean, it's a legendary battle. . . ." He saw her blank expression, stammered, and said, "I thought you'd know about famous battles, what with . . . that is . . ." He saw the growing anger in her expression and decided to stop without finishing the sentence—but he couldn't help looking at the ridged brow-plate that was the most visible sign of her Klingon ancestry.

"What would I know about battles?" Torres shouted, grabbing the crewman by the front of his uniform and lifting him off the floor. "I'm an engineer, dammit, not a soldier!"

Just then the ship shook under another Hachai barrage, and Torres tossed the crewman aside and hurried to tend her engines.

The crewman, unhurt, picked himself up off the floor and stared at Torres, amazed that someone that size, even a Klingon, could be strong enough to throw him around like that. She wasn't very big at all, considerably smaller than he was, but she had lifted him without any apparent effort.

Klingons were apparently stronger than they looked. Given how formidable many of them looked, that was a rather frightening thought.

He brushed himself off and muttered to one of the Engineering crew, "I thought *all* Klingons studied battles and warrior myths."

The engineer glanced surreptitiously at Torres. "She's only half-Klingon," he whispered back. "She was raised on Earth, and she likes to favor her human side. Doesn't like it when people take her for a full Klingon."

"Well, she's got Klingon strength and a Klingon *temper,* anyway."

"Don't tell *her* that!"

The crewman nodded; he didn't want to find himself on the floor again—or worse.

Besides, he was supposed to get back up to the bridge with his report.

On the bridge, at that moment, Janeway demanded, "Assessment of the situation, Mr. Tuvok."

"Our own circumstances are precarious, Captain," the Vulcan replied, as he turned to read one of the wall displays. "Due to the superiority of the P'nir shield technology over Hachai offensive weaponry, the Hachai are accustomed to operating by englobement, and have pursued that tactic against us, making it impossible for us to simply retreat the way we came. We must instead maneuver for survival, while looking for openings in the Hachai formations. Such openings are inevitable, but it is not inevitable, nor even probable, that they will allow us immediate escape from the conflict; it's more likely that we will need to find our way through several partial englobements before breaking into open space."

"Is that going to be a serious problem?" Janeway asked. "You said we could hold out for hours."

"That depends on what methods you choose to employ, and on the attitude of the P'nir," Tuvok replied, turning to face her across the pale gray console that separated his station from the central level of the bridge. "If we do not return fire, the Hachai will be able to close in more tightly on us; if we fight, the Hachai will presumably be forced to keep their distance, and openings will therefore be more likely to occur, but we can expect heavier concentrations of fire directed at us in return. Our perceived willingness not to merely fend off, but if necessary to destroy, Hachai ships will also affect the outcome."

"We'll do what we have to," Janeway replied. "What was that about the P'nir attitude?"

Tuvok explained, "While we must assume that the Hachai will be uniformly hostile, we do not yet know whether the P'nir will ignore us, or aid us, or perhaps even join the Hachai in attacking us."

"I should think they'd be willing to help us," Janeway said. "Isn't there an old saying, 'My enemy's enemy is my friend'?"

"As with so many of your human proverbs, Captain," Tuvok said, "there is a counter to that— 'Better the devil you know than the devil you do not.'"

"Well, then, let's let the P'nir know who we are," Janeway snapped. She glanced forward; Paris was far too busy keeping *Voyager* clear of Hachai attacks to be bothered. She looked to port and saw that Kim's station was vacant.

"Get someone in here to take over in Ops," she called. Then she turned back to starboard. "Tuvok," she said, "see if you can open a channel to the P'nir."

"Aye-aye."

Janeway watched the main viewscreen as weapons fire blossomed vividly across their shields. The image wheeled and veered as Paris maneuvered the ship.

"The P'nir are refusing our hail, Captain," the Vulcan reported.

"Damn," Janeway said.

The ship shook as a Hachai blast struck it squarely.

"Shields at ninety-four percent, Captain," Tuvok reported. "Mr. Paris, if you will notice . . ."

"The gap ahead, starboard," Paris replied. "I see it, thanks."

"Captain, should we return fire?" Tuvok asked.

"How does it affect our odds?" Janeway demanded.

"Due to the fact that it will make us more dangerous and cause the Hachai to concentrate greater effort on us, our odds of destruction in each encounter will increase," Tuvok said. "However, because our weapons should cause the Hachai to keep their distance, the odds of escape from any given attempt at entrapment also improve. The net result is that fighting will not significantly change the odds of our survival and eventual freedom, but will accelerate the outcome, whichever it may prove to be."

"It'll make whatever's going to happen happen faster," Janeway said.

"Yes," Tuvok said. "And it may also affect the attitudes of both the Hachai and the P'nir toward us. We have insufficient data on their respective psychologies to determine just what that effect might be."

"Well, we're not in any hurry yet, not while the shields are still solid," Janeway said. She stared at the blazing inferno on the viewscreen, considering, then asked, "Since we're in here anyway, can we get a closer look at that globe?"

"I don't think so," Paris replied. "I don't have a

lot of choice about where we go, Captain, not if I want to keep us in one piece."

"The unidentified object is not in our immediate vicinity," Tuvok said. "I must agree with Lieutenant Paris—any attempt to approach it would significantly decrease our odds of survival."

Janeway nodded. It had been worth asking. Another thought struck her. "Mr. Tuvok, the P'nir aren't willing to talk to us, but what *are* they doing? How are they reacting to our presence? Are they moving into position against us?"

"On the contrary," Tuvok reported. "The Hachai have diverted their resources slightly in order to deal with us, and the P'nir, having noted this, are shifting their own concentration toward the far side of the battle zone. If the Hachai continue to devote significant effort against us, the P'nir advantage at the far side of the conflict may become decisive."

"You mean the P'nir might win the whole thing because the Hachai are busy shooting at us?" Janeway demanded. "We may have altered the outcome just by being here?"

"Exactly, Captain. You will recall that you described the battle as a chaotic system."

"And in a chaotic system, the tiniest change can affect the outcome," Janeway said. She glared angrily at the screen. "So we may have given the P'nir the eventual victory, just by being here—but meanwhile they aren't doing a thing to help us in return."

"No, they are not," the Vulcan confirmed. "In fact, from their positions, I would judge that the P'nir expect the *Voyager* to be destroyed, and they are maneuvering to be able to take advantage of the momentary disorganization the Hachai will experience when that occurs."

"Contact the Hachai," Janeway ordered. "Tell them what the P'nir are doing. Show them your findings."

"Hailing."

The main viewer could not be diverted for communications, not while Paris was flying the ship through the thick of the battle, so the channel to the Hachai was through Tuvok's station; Janeway did not turn to see the visual, but she listened to the audio.

"More *thagn* P'nir treachery!" the Hachai commander shouted angrily. "Do you really think we didn't see something that obvious? Of course we see it! But it's a trick—*you* are the real threat!"

When the transmission was cut off, Janeway said, "I heard, Tuvok." She frowned, watching the screen unhappily. It seemed as if every time Paris aimed the ship at open space, a Hachai dreadnought would appear from nowhere, cutting them off, weapons blazing.

If they continued trying to dodge and run the Hachai would wear them down slowly, and despite Paris's evident piloting skills, despite Tuvok's estimation of the odds, it seemed to Janeway that eventually the *Voyager* would be caught and destroyed.

If destruction was inevitable, she wasn't going to go down without a fight. And if they had already given one side the victory, they might as well make sure that it was a decisive one, one that would leave the winners in a condition to someday recover. That might mean a P'nir fleet would come out of the Kuriyar Cluster looking for trouble, but at least it would mean that the P'nir would survive.

"It seems the Hachai really *want* a war, and the one against the P'nir isn't enough for them," Janeway said at last. She reached down and wiped away the smear of dust where the Hachai doll had lain, then straightened up again.

"If that's what they want, let's give them one," she said. "Mr. Tuvok, you have a free hand, as far as the Hachai are concerned—you may fire at will."

CHAPTER
18

HARRY KIM SMILED NERVOUSLY TO HIMSELF AS HE stood alone in the darkness. At last he had found the door. He could feel its outline clearly.

He hadn't found any latch he could work, not even when he felt up and down both sides from knee level to the top of his head, but he could handle that; he aimed his phaser carefully and pressed the trigger.

The beam's red glare and the shower of sparks were blinding after so long in total darkness; Kim blinked, then squinted, his free hand shielding his eyes. The smell of melting metal mingled with the oily stench the air already had to make a truly revolting odor.

Unlike many cultures, the P'nir apparently did

not build their doors to default to open when damaged; the door didn't move when the beam struck it. Kim released the trigger and lowered his weapon, then waited for his eyes to readjust.

The darkness was no longer absolute, even when the phaser had cooled and its glow vanished. The beam had cut a small hole through the door, and whatever was on the other side of it was lit; the ugly green glow of P'nir lighting seeped in through the tiny opening, providing Kim with enough light to make out, dimly, his surroundings.

Kim took a minute to look around, hoping that no one would happen to see the hole while he did it.

He still couldn't identify the round things on the far side of the room; they looked like sacks of some sort. There wasn't anything else in the place—he could see no furniture of any kind.

He did finally spot what he took to be the door controls, and maybe even a light switch, built into the doorframe a dozen centimeters above his head. He hadn't checked that far up when he had felt around before.

The P'nir, he decided, must be very tall indeed.

He peered up at the panel, but he didn't have enough light to make it out clearly, and he didn't want to just experiment randomly.

There wasn't any obvious way to get the door open. He sighed, and set to work slicing out a panel large enough for him to crawl through.

When the panel came free he caught it an instant

before it would have rattled onto the floor, and lowered it gently—and silently. He looked through the opening, hoping that he wasn't going to find a squad of P'nir security guards waiting out there for him.

He saw no feet, no shadows, no sign that anyone was nearby; he knelt and crawled through.

He was in a passageway, about the width of an ordinary corridor, but much taller; he scrambled to his feet and looked both ways.

The walls and decks were mostly smooth, featureless black; the ceiling seemed to be lost in the greenish gloom overhead. Far above him on the walls, were red and green markings he could not interpret.

There were closed doors all along one side of the corridor; he had just cut his way through one of them. The opposite side was blank.

This was one of the gloomiest, most ominous places he had ever seen in his life, Kim thought.

He tried to remember the scan he had seen of the P'nir ship, and to figure out which direction would lead to the hangar deck. He'd become disoriented in the unlit storeroom, but he thought that he remembered which side of the corridor the room had been on . . . but he wasn't sure.

Well, if he was wrong, he'd just have to get turned around later. He picked his direction and started walking, moving as quietly as he could, his phaser ready in his hand.

He'd gone a hundred meters along the passageway and rounded two corners before he finally remembered to reset his weapon to stun.

"Activate emergency medical hologram!" Kes shouted, as she helped a wounded crewman, dazed and staggering, in through the door of sickbay.

She had been on her way back up to the bridge, to ask if she could help, when she had found this man slumped against a corridor wall, bleeding profusely from a head wound and seemingly unable to move any farther under his own power. She had grabbed him by the arm and almost dragged him here.

The familiar image of the doctor appeared instantly beside one of the beds, facing the wrong direction. "Please state the nature of the medical emergency," he said, as he turned to see the Ocampa and the crewman.

Blood was streaming from a gash in the man's forehead; Kes didn't bother to answer the hologram's standard preprogrammed question.

The doctor didn't seem to need an answer. "Get him on the bed," the hologram ordered.

Kes struggled to obey, but the dazed crewman was much larger and heavier than she was and was not helping much. The doctor reappeared at her side and grabbed the man's legs, heaving him gently but unceremoniously into position.

Amazing, Kes thought, that computer-generated magnetic fields could work so much like human hands.

"What happened to him?" the hologram asked as he ran a medical scanner over the head wound. "A drunken brawl in the lounge?"

"No," Kes replied. "I think he fell and hit his head on some equipment."

"Mmm," the hologram said. "Severe scalp laceration and a minor concussion. We can fix that right up. Though I'm not sure it's wise for us to be encouraging such clumsiness." He was working on the wound even as he spoke, running a tissue sealer along the gash.

"He wasn't clumsy," Kes protested.

"Oh? Then how did he come . . ." the hologram began.

Just then the ship shuddered as a Hachai barrage assaulted the shields.

The doctor looked up at the ceiling as if he expected it to fall in on them at any second. "What was that?" he demanded.

"We're under attack," Kes explained. "That was how he fell."

"Under attack?" the hologram asked, staring at her. "By whom?"

"They're called the Hachai," Kes explained. "We got caught up in a big battle between them and these people called the P'nir."

"Oh, did we?" The hologram frowned as he made a final pass along the wound with his instrument. "Perhaps it was the captain who was clumsy, then," he said.

"Perhaps," Kes said quietly.

The doctor put the tissue sealer aside and began

wiping away the blood with a cleansing pad. "Should I expect more casualties?"

"I don't know," Kes admitted. "Probably."

"The battle is continuing?"

"Oh, yes. Mr. Tuvok said it would last another thirty years."

The hologram abruptly stopped and put down the pad. He looked at his patient, then at Kes.

"This hardly seems like an appropriate time for jokes," he said reprovingly.

"I'm not joking, Doctor," Kes replied.

"Well, somebody must be," the doctor said, "and it hardly seems likely that it's Tuvok! He's a Vulcan, for heaven's sake—Vulcans don't joke."

"No one's joking," Kes said quietly.

"Nonsense," the hologram insisted. "Space battles do not last for thirty years! My programming directs me to assume that absurd statements made by persons who are not likely to be delirious are attempts at humor, and I would say that *your* statement certainly qualifies as absurd."

Then he paused and stared at Kes, as if struck by a new thought. "Or are you delirious? Did *you* bump your head, as well?"

She shook her head. "No, I'm fine, Doctor."

"Then don't tell me these silly tales of thirty-year battles!"

"I'm afraid it's true," Kes insisted. "Ask the captain if you don't believe me."

The doctor stared at her for a moment, then said, "I'll just do that." He looked up. "Sickbay to bridge."

"Janeway here. We're rather busy right now, Doctor—what is it?"

"This Ocampa woman is here with some foolishness about a thirty-year battle. . . ."

"We're in a battle right now, Doctor, and yes, it could last thirty years—but *we* won't, if we don't get out of here. Bridge out."

The doctor stared at the ceiling for a moment, then turned back to Kes.

"You were serious," he said.

She nodded.

"And the captain was serious?"

Kes nodded again.

"We might be destroyed?"

"It's possible," Kes said. "Though I certainly hope we won't be—they're trying to get us clear."

"In any case, we can expect more casualties, can't we? Before we're destroyed, I mean."

"I think so," Kes agreed.

"Well, then what are you standing there for?" the doctor shouted. "This man's condition is stabilized—get the next bed ready! Bring me a medical tricorder, and make sure we still have internal transporter capability to get the wounded here. . . ."

The hologram began readying his own supplies, checking the computer log of what was on hand against what was actually in the various compartments.

"I assume you're available to help me out—what about . . ." The doctor paused, and seemed to shudder, though Kes thought that might just be a power fluctuation in the imaging systems. "What about Lieutenant Paris? Not that he was all that much help."

"Oh, he's at the helm," Kes said. "He can't possibly leave his post."

The doctor nodded, and Kes almost thought he looked relieved. "I see," he said. "And I suppose the rest of the crew is all busy at battle stations, as well, and there aren't any surplus personnel we could recruit to assist us?"

"I don't know," Kes said. "I suppose Neelix might be . . . I mean, the captain ordered him off the bridge, told him to go cook."

"Neelix? The Talaxian?"

Kes nodded.

The hologram appeared to consider the idea carefully; Kes was once again amazed at how lifelike the simulation of a human being was.

"I don't think anyone's going to be interested in food during a battle—at least, not for the first few hours," the hologram said. "Get him down here. If he gets in the way we can always send him back to his pots and pans."

Kes nodded, and tapped her combadge.

As she summoned Neelix, she thought to herself that it would be a relief having him there; she wouldn't have to worry about what might be happening to him elsewhere.

Then she glanced at the doctor. Had *he* thought of that? *Could* he have thought of that? Had he decided Neelix should be here not because he would really be helpful, but just so Kes wouldn't worry?

She didn't know. Federation technology was a wonderful thing, but could a computer program have been so thoughtful as that?

She decided not to worry about it. It didn't really matter why, so long as Neelix would be there with her.

Just then the ship shook violently. A moment later the shimmer of a transporter appeared over one of the beds, and the first of the next batch of wounded appeared. Kes hurried to help.

When Neelix arrived a few minutes later he found Kes and the doctor working together over a badly burned woman—a power conduit had blown out on Deck Eight.

The Talaxian watched helplessly for a moment, then responded to the call of another of the injured.

As he tried to soothe the flash-blinded crewman, Neelix stole another glance at Kes and the doctor, still working smoothly together.

How could she work so well, Neelix wondered, with a mere holographic image? The two of them were moving smoothly together, Kes handing the doctor the right item almost before his hand reached out for it.

That sort of easy cooperation usually came from years of close contact, among people who worked together constantly—or in old married couples.

Neelix frowned at that.

Could it be some manifestation of Kes's psychic abilities? Did she have some sort of telepathic rapport with the holographic doctor?

How could she have any sort of psychic link to a mere machine?

And as he patted cooling antiseptic onto abrasions, Neelix wondered whether he, himself, could possibly be *jealous* of a holographic image.

CHAPTER
19

CHAKOTAY AND ROLLINS HAD BEEN SITTING CROSS-legged on the dark brown steel floor, talking quietly, and Bereyt had been lounging comfortably against a black wall, when an electric crackle drew the first officer's attention. He looked up as the forcefield in the doorway vanished.

The single P'nir who stood in the opening had a broad stripe of yellowish green across the full width of its chest—in the dim green light Chakotay couldn't tell whether the color was paint, or some sort of stretched fabric, or something else entirely. He supposed that however it had been applied, it might be an indicator of rank.

It wasn't anything they had seen before, at any

rate, and it did serve to distinguish this P'nir from the ones that had brought them to this cell.

Chakotay did not bother to stand; even if he had, he still would have had to crane his neck to meet the P'nir's eyes. Instead he simply turned his head and looked up.

"Tell me how your larger ship is armed," the P'nir demanded, without preamble. The question did not seem to be addressed to anyone in particular, but with that blank face and the pupilless eyes it was hard to be certain. The creature was looking down at the three captives, but Chakotay could not say which of them, if any, it had focused on.

Rollins and Bereyt looked to Chakotay for guidance; Chakotay had been ready for this. "We wish to speak to your captain," he replied immediately.

The P'nir stared down at him with those four red eyes. Its hard, featureless face couldn't change expression, but Chakotay thought it managed to look annoyed anyway.

"Tell me how your larger ship is armed," it repeated, a little louder.

"Sir," Bereyt said, leaning over toward Chakotay, "have you noticed that these people always speak in imperatives?"

Chakotay threw her a startled glance, and realized that she was right. The only times he'd gotten a response from a P'nir he had prefaced a question with "Tell me."

That might be helpful. Perhaps he could communicate with these beings after all. He unfolded his legs and got slowly to his feet, then looked up at the P'nir.

"Take us to your captain!" he demanded.

"No," the P'nir said. "Tell me how your larger ship is armed."

That reply wasn't exactly cooperative, but the P'nir had at least responded to him; Bereyt's observation had been accurate. The P'nir were apparently disinterested in any sort of polite implication. His statement that they wanted to speak to the captain had been ignored as irrelevant, while a demand to see the captain had at least gotten an answer. He had to tell the P'nir outright what he wanted in order to get them to pay any attention at all.

"Understand that I'm forbidden to tell you that," he said, raising his head high and trying to look as commanding as he could.

That wasn't very commanding at all, when faced with a creature a meter taller than himself; he felt almost like a child, looking up at the thing's face.

The P'nir stared down at him.

"Tell me who forbids it," it said.

"My own captain forbids it."

"Defy your captain."

Chakotay stared up at the P'nir for a moment, considering that, then said, "Only a captain has the right to defy a captain. Isn't that . . . I mean, tell me whether that is true among the P'nir."

The P'nir stared down at him and seemed to think for a moment before replying.

"It is not true," it said.

"Explain," Chakotay snapped back instantly.

The P'nir seemed uncomfortable; perhaps it was unsettled by the reversal of roles, by Chakotay making demands instead of yielding to them. Still, it answered.

"One may defy a captain not one's own," the P'nir said. "And when a captain acts improperly, even one's own captain must be defied."

"*My* captain has certainly not acted improperly," Chakotay said.

"Your captain is not P'nir," the P'nir replied. "Your captain is not a true captain."

Chakotay frowned—he supposed that the P'nir wouldn't recognize the expression; after all, the P'nir had no facial expressions themselves, and had not dealt face-to-face with any other intelligent species for centuries.

"Tell me how you know that my captain is not P'nir," he said.

The P'nir was definitely uncomfortable now; two of its arms were swaying about oddly, as if looking for something for its claws to grab. Perhaps, Chakotay thought, arm motions served the same purpose among the P'nir that facial expressions served among humanoids.

"Your captain is no true captain," the P'nir said.

"Tell me how you *know* that," Chakotay insisted.

"Your captain acted improperly," it said. "No P'nir captain would act so improperly."

"Tell me how my captain acted improperly," Chakotay said. "I do not see any improper action."

"Your captain sent you into danger," the P'nir

replied. "Your captain betrayed you. You are here, among us, against your will—a true captain protects her underlings and does not send them to the domains of others without agreement. Obey K't'rien, the captain of the ship you are on—and obey me, her representative!"

This explanation and demand provided Chakotay with an interesting look at the P'nir culture, but he did not take the time to pursue it; he wanted to maintain whatever conversational advantage he had at the moment.

"No," he said. "I will not obey you. My captain's act was not improper."

"Then your captain is no P'nir!"

Chakotay could not very well argue any further with that, under the circumstances.

"*I* am no P'nir!" he said.

"Then you are nothing. Tell me how your captain's ship is armed," the P'nir demanded.

"No. Take me to your captain," Chakotay responded.

"No."

That brought the conversation to a halt.

Stalemate.

Chakotay tried to think of some way to convey to the P'nir that maybe, just maybe, Chakotay would be more cooperative with the captain than with this underling—assuming that this *was* a mere underling; the green stripe might well mark it as an officer. It could well be the ship's first officer, his own counterpart.

It wasn't the captain, though; it had said as

much, had said it was merely the captain's representative.

How could he convince it that he would obey the captain, when he would not obey the captain's representative?

He could not devise any way to suggest such a thing in a way that the P'nir would accept and yet that wouldn't be an outright lie.

He could tell a lie, of course—but he had the impression that a people as direct as the P'nir would not take kindly to liars.

Or would they? That was jumping to conclusions. They seemed to be quite adept at lying to the Hachai, to go by the intense Hachai fear of "P'nir trickery."

But they were at war with the Hachai, which might make anything fair, as far as they were concerned. The Hachai were the enemy. Perhaps the P'nir saw no point in treating enemies honorably.

He didn't think the P'nir would appreciate anyone lying to the P'nir, though. They didn't seem to be very strong on the idea of reciprocity.

At least, he thought, this one didn't; others might be more reasonable.

He glanced at Bereyt, but she didn't seem to have any suggestions this time.

Before he could look at Rollins, or turn back to the P'nir, the P'nir turned away, and the forcefield reappeared; apparently it had taken the movement of his head as a sign that the discussion was at an end.

Chakotay glowered after it.

"Damn," he said. "How am I supposed to negotiate with creatures with an attitude like that?"

"I don't know, sir," Bereyt replied. "I thought you did rather well, considering."

"Not well enough," Chakotay said.

"It may not be possible to do any better," Bereyt said. "The Hachai don't seem to have managed it, in all these hundreds of years."

"We don't know if they *tried* to negotiate," Chakotay objected.

"Well, you tried, sir," Rollins suggested. "Maybe Captain Janeway will do better."

At that moment, aboard the *Voyager*, Janeway ordered, "No torpedoes. We can't resupply."

"I would point out, Captain," Tuvok said, "that if we die here, conserving our photon torpedoes will have been of no benefit whatsoever."

"I know that, Tuvok," Janeway snapped. "We'll get out of here—and we'll do it without using up any more photon torpedoes. Is that clear?"

"Abundantly clear, Captain," the Vulcan said. "Firing phasers."

The statement was hardly necessary; the flare of the *Voyager*'s weapons was obvious, a vivid line of orange-red on the screen. It struck the shields of the Hachai dreadnought that had been harassing them; the shields fluoresced blue-green, and phaser energy dissipated in a cloud of superheated interstellar hydrogen and glittering metal dust, the dust of the hundreds of ships that had been destroyed in the centuries the battle had raged.

And that was all that happened. The blast didn't penetrate the Hachai ship's shields at all. The dreadnought was still coming after them.

"Evasive action, Mr. Paris," Janeway called.

"Aye-aye, Captain," Paris replied, as he threw the *Voyager* into a sliding movement to one side.

"Continue firing, Mr. Tuvok."

"Firing phasers."

Again the fiery red beams lashed out, and again they spattered into useless heat and light against the Hachai dreadnought's shields.

"It would seem that Mr. Neelix was correct about the efficacy of Hachai shield generators, Captain," Tuvok said. "Our weapons are having no effect whatsoever."

"So I see," Janeway replied. "And if Neelix knew that, I wonder if he knows any way to defeat them?"

"I would not consider it likely, Captain, given his extreme reluctance to encounter the Hachai," the Vulcan said.

"True," Janeway said, but even so, she called, "Neelix to the bridge, please."

"Captain, this is the emergency medical hologram," came the reply. "Mr. Neelix is assisting with the wounded; is his presence on the bridge essential?"

Shaken, Janeway looked up. She hadn't realized there were wounded already, but of course there would be—she'd heard the damage reports, and any time the ride got rough enough to damage equipment, it was rough enough to damage people, as well. "Doctor, how many wounded are there?"

"We have eight so far, Captain—none of them critical."

Just then the ship shook as a Hachai assault struck with sufficient force to be felt through the shields.

"Mr. Neelix," Janeway called, "our weapons aren't penetrating the Hachai shields. Do you know of any way to change that?"

"I'm afraid not, Captain," the Talaxian replied. "That's why the Hachai shield generators were always such a popular trade item."

"Thank you, Mr. Neelix," Janeway replied. "Continue to assist in sickbay, please; bridge out."

Then she turned to the Vulcan. "Tactical analysis, Mr. Tuvok," she said.

"The only discernable effect of our fire has been to antagonize the Hachai," Tuvok reported. "The ineffectuality of our phasers has been obvious, and the Hachai are therefore not bothering to keep their distance. We are, Captain, in serious peril."

"Is there anything we can do about it?"

"If we are once clear of the combat zone, we can escape easily," Tuvok replied. "Sensor analysis indicates that neither the Hachai nor the P'nir vessels are capable of true warp speeds. However, unless Mr. Paris can extricate us from the combat zone, or we can find a weapon that is effective against Hachai shields and force an opening, I see no way to achieve this escape. We are trapped within the sphere of conflict, and I would estimate that within six hours our power reserves will be exhausted, our shields will fail, and the *Voyager* will be destroyed."

Janeway turned to look at the viewscreen; they were passing terrifyingly close to the broadside of a Hachai dreadnought just then, the immense gray surface banded with three orange stripes filling the entire image. Then they were past it, heading toward a trio of dark, jagged P'nir ships—and the bridge trembled as the Hachai dreadnought fired on them.

"'Find a weapon that is effective against Hachai shields,'" Janeway said, as she leaned on the forward console and stared at the main viewer. "The Hachai shields are more efficient than our own, you said, Mr. Tuvok—why?"

"Because, Captain," Tuvok explained, "they are much more finely tuned than ours. The Hachai do not waste energy defending against impossible attacks, or in letting shields on a single ship interfere with each other; each ship uses a single integrated energy field wherein every erg they put into their shields is in the frequency range and resonance patterns of which P'nir weaponry is capable, while our own shields are less discriminating."

"And the P'nir can't build weapons in other ranges or patterns?"

"Apparently not. The range of effectiveness of the Hachai shields, while less than our own, is still extremely broad."

"And the P'nir can't tune their weapons outside that range," Janeway said. "But they're not using phasers. They don't have Kawamura-Franklin circuitry; their weapons aren't monopolarically phased."

"This is true, Captain," the Vulcan acknowledged. "But I fail to see how it benefits us."

"I don't know if it does, Tuvok—but I'm not an engineer." She straightened up and called, "Janeway to Engineering."

"Torres here, Captain. If you're wondering about the engines . . ."

"Not this time, B'Elanna," Janeway said. "I trust you to keep the engines going as best you can."

Torres sighed. "What do you need?" She couldn't stop herself from adding, "I'm pretty busy down here, Captain, trying to keep up with this battering."

"B'Elanna, I want you to look at the sensor readouts on the Hachai shields, and see if you can find any way we can get through them," Janeway explained. "These people don't have phasers; their weapons aren't monopolaric. Is there any way we can use that?"

"Captain, I've been nursing the engines along down here, and the way Mr. Paris is abusing them, I haven't been thinking about . . ."

Just then the entire ship was jarred by a Hachai energy barrage; Janeway lurched as the bridge seemed to tilt beneath her. The viewscreen flickered, and the lights dimmed; for half a second the only illumination was the blue and gold glow of the control panels.

"B'Elanna, if we don't find a way to get through those shields soon," Janeway said, "we may not *have* any engines! Let Carey handle the engines; you get to work on cracking those shields!"

CHAPTER

20

HARRY KIM CROUCHED BY THE BULKHEAD, WISHING HE could hold his breath for more than a minute or two at a time; his phaser was ready in his hand, pointed at the distant ceiling, but he really, truly hoped he wouldn't need it.

The rattlings and thumpings around the curve in the passageway seemed to go on and on interminably, as the P'nir went about their business—whatever it was.

Kim had no idea what was going on; he was just waiting for the sounds to move away.

And they hadn't moved.

So he was still crouching, still waiting.

He had yet to actually see one of the P'nir, even

here; he hadn't risked looking around the curve at them.

He had been creeping down this passage, and he had heard the sounds and had frozen. Then he had carefully, quietly crept to this dim corner and had waited, hoping that whatever the P'nir were doing would not bring them around the curve where they would see him.

And he was still waiting.

He wished he had some way to cover up his face and the shoulders of his uniform; he thought the rest would blend into the black of the corridor walls.

He wondered how acute the P'nir's hearing was.

He wondered what they looked like. Judging by what he had seen of the ship, especially the wall-markings and the little control panels in the door-frames, he assumed that the P'nir were considerably taller than human beings. Judging by the sounds he now heard, he also thought that they probably had hard claws, rather than soft fingers.

That really shouldn't affect his opinion of them as people, he told himself. Starfleet taught its cadets to ignore the mere physical appearance of a sentient being as completely as possible, and to concentrate on the mind and soul within. A gaseous intelligence from inside a star could well be a spiritual brother; Kim knew that.

However, he still didn't like the sound of all those claws clicking and snapping, just around the curve. Some primitive part of him couldn't help imagining those claws biting into *him,* and he found himself quite irrationally disliking the P'nir, sight unseen.

He considered trying to slip away, back to the storeroom where he had arrived, but quickly rejected the idea; by now P'nir security might well have discovered the hole he had cut in the door.

He had passed other corridors; he thought about backtracking and trying one of those. The passage he was in seemed to be headed in the right direction, but perhaps he'd be safer finding a less-direct route.

The more he thought about it, and the longer those nasty clicking noises continued, the better the idea of an alternate route seemed, until at last, moving with all the stealth he could manage, he slipped back down the passage and then into one of the smaller side corridors.

" 'Let Carey handle the engines,' " Torres muttered to herself as she prepared to turn the systems over to her fellow engineer.

"Carey couldn't handle a warp drive properly if you imprinted the instructions directly into his neurons! The man can't realign a plasma conduit to save his life." She turned to glare at the shimmering blue glow of the warp core.

"You behave yourself!" she shouted at the machinery. "You just stay aligned, or I'll take you apart with my bare hands, space the pieces, and build the ship a new warp drive myself!"

That outburst made her feel a little better. She

turned and shouted, "Mr. Carey! I need to work on something else—see if you can keep these engines on line!"

Lieutenant Carey hurried to the main engine panel without a word.

That silent cooperation made her feel even better, and she wasn't really frowning anymore as she crossed to a computer access screen and summoned up Tuvok's analysis of the Hachai shields.

Elegant three-dimensional waveforms danced across the display, and in spite of herself Torres found herself caught up in analyzing them.

Those shields were beautiful work, she thought—absolutely wonderful design. The Hachai clearly included some top-rate engineers if they were able to build things that could put up defensive fields like this. The energy flow was absolutely smooth, with none of the complex and wasteful heterodyne effects of ordinary shields.

In fact, Torres thought, there was virtually no energy waste at all; the standing fields wouldn't draw a tenth the power that the *Voyager*'s shields did, and ordinarily they'd probably be able to absorb a hundred times the punishment.

Of course, that lovely smoothness meant that the fields would all be synchronized, lined up on top of each other, and if you could get a phaser beam's polarization to match that synchronization it would go right through as if the shield weren't there.

That realization brought back a memory from her year at Starfleet Academy.

There was a reason that no one back in the Alpha Quadrant built shields like this. It wasn't that they'd never *thought* of aligning the fields, Torres remembered. That had been a fairly obvious notion, and had been suggested many times over the past century or so.

The problem with any such setup was that vulnerability to the right polarization—and it was a pretty major problem. After all, every so often you'd get that synchronicity just by chance, in normal use, and you could expect any intelligent enemy to find ways to do it on purpose. Those smooth curves were efficient, but they did have that flaw.

And of *course* you could find ways to do it on purpose. It ought to be easy.

In fact, thinking about it . . .

Could it really be *that* simple?

She frowned, and called, "Torres to Janeway— you said these people aren't using phasers?"

"No," the captain replied. "They're using nonpolarized phased energy."

"Then they must be using a lot of power behind them, right?" Torres asked. "These shields Tuvok is showing me would be better than ninety-nine-percent effective against anything like that."

On the bridge, Janeway turned questioningly to Tuvok.

"That does seem to be the case," the Vulcan confirmed. "Based on our observations, the effectiveness of P'nir energy weapons against Hachai shields would appear to be less than one-tenth of one percent."

"And that's still more than we're doing," Janeway said. "Have you got something, B'Elanna?"

"Well, I think so, Captain, but I can't believe it could be that simple."

"What?"

"Well, the *weapons* aren't polarized, but the *shields* are," Torres explained. "That's what makes them so efficient. So if you were to rotate the polarity of the phasers until it matched the polarity of the shields, they ought to go right through as if the shields weren't there at all."

Janeway looked at Tuvok, but he gave no sign of comprehension.

"Yes, that's all very well in theory," Janeway said, "but how do we know what the polarity of the shields *is,* in order to match it? We can't very well take the time to scan each individual ship's shields as it moves in to attack, and analyze the polarity, and align our phasers to match."

"Oh, that's the easy part, Captain," Torres replied. "Since shields absorb whatever energy is directed at them, and phasers are all polarized to begin with, if you fire a phaser at the shields the energy flow of the shields will warp into the opposite alignment as it absorbs the phaser energy. All you have to do then is reverse the polarity on the phasers. And since it'll go right through, the shields won't be absorbing any of the energy, so they won't realign—you'll be able to cut the shielded ship apart as if it were so much cheese."

Janeway and Tuvok exchanged stares.

The ship lurched, and Paris muttered curses to himself as he threw *Voyager* out of the line of fire.

"You heard her, Mr. Tuvok," Janeway said. "Pick your target and fire when ready."

"Yes, Captain," Tuvok replied.

Janeway watched, tense, as the Vulcan scanned the *Voyager*'s surroundings.

"Target selected," he said. "Phasers locked on."

"Fire!" Janeway barked, as she whirled to look at the viewscreen.

The red line of fire lashed out and spattered against the shields of the immense Hachai vessel. The shields flared greenish-blue. . . .

"Reversing polarity," Tuvok said calmly.

For an instant, Janeway saw no change; the *Voyager*'s phaser beam was still vanishing into blue-green radiance against the shields.

And then the phasers punched right through the Hachai ship's shields and drew a line of fire across the fuselage, slicing the metal of the hull and heating either side of the gash red-hot, and incidentally shearing away an antenna caught in the searing beam.

An instant later the warship's inner hull gave way under the phaser's assault, spraying forth a growing cloud of gas and debris. An exhaust port blew out several meters away from the cut as the ship's internal pressure collapsed, and a gout of dark matter spouted from there, as well.

"Cease fire!" Janeway shouted.

The beam vanished.

The damaged Hachai ship was already wheeling, however, turning aside to escape this unexpectedly deadly attack, breaking formation and sending its own allies into disarray. Wreckage was spilling from the long gouge in its side.

Janeway felt slightly ill. They had come here to make peace, not to destroy. She wondered what sort of casualties the Hachai had sustained just then; few, she hoped.

"Engineering," Janeway snapped. "B'Elanna, did you see that?"

"Yes, Captain," Torres replied. "It looks as if it worked. Those overtuned shields aren't going to be much use against our phasers anymore."

Before either woman could say another word, the *Voyager* shook under a sudden attack; the main viewer blanked out for a moment, overloaded.

"Six Hachai vessels are concentrating fire on us, Captain," Tuvok reported. "Shields at eighty-eight percent."

"Return fire, Mr. Tuvok," Janeway said. "And reverse polarity as necessary." She hesitated, then added, "Concentrate on drive systems and armament, and avoid life-support; we want them disabled, but we don't want to kill anyone unnecessarily."

"Understood, Captain," Tuvok said. "Firing phasers."

Janeway leaned forward, a hand on the helm console, for a better look at the screen as the image was restored, filtered down so that it could be seen clearly.

The console was hot beneath her hand; the ship's systems were straining. She unconsciously absorbed that information and added it to the factors already being weighed as she studied the screen.

Another Hachai ship was being hit; she couldn't make out the details in the degraded image visible through their own overworked shields, but she could see that once again the phasers were dissipating harmlessly.

"Reversing polarity," Tuvok said, and an instant later it was obvious that the attack had penetrated. Molten scraps sprayed from the side of the Hachai vessel as the phasers sheared easily through the hull.

Janeway smiled a tight, unhappy little smile.

The *Voyager*'s weapons could, indeed, pierce the Hachai screens, if they could be held on their targets long enough to use Torres's polarity-reversing trick. The need for sustained contact meant that they couldn't just rip the Hachai ships apart at will, though; they would have to settle for inflicting relatively light damage.

Which was all to the good, if it meant they wouldn't be killing large numbers of the Hachai. And even that was more than Janeway had expected—and more than the Hachai had expected, as well, she was sure. Neelix had said that the Hachai knew they built the best shields in this sector of the galaxy; they would have been confident of their safety from this strange intruder, and now that confidence would be shaken. . . .

Janeway turned and started to call to Harry Kim to open a channel, and remembered before the first word left her lips that Harry wasn't there, he was with Chakotay aboard one of the P'nir cruisers. Tuvok was busy with fire control; Paris was trying to guide the ship out of the battle. A man she barely knew, a Maquis named Evans, was now filling in in Ops.

The ship shuddered violently as another Hachai barrage struck.

"Mr. Evans," Janeway called. "Open a channel to the Hachai."

"Hailing the Hachai, Captain," Evans replied.

The *Voyager*'s phasers flashed out again, and after a second or two of ineffectual sputtering, they abruptly cut into the side of a Hachai destroyer.

"Cease fire, Mr. Tuvok," Janeway said. "Mr. Evans, do you have a channel?"

"I think so, Captain," Evans replied. "They're not answering, but I think they're listening."

Janeway nodded. "Good enough."

She stood facing the main screen and announced, "This is Captain Kathryn Janeway, of the Federation starship *Voyager*. You have seen that our weapons are effective against you, despite your best defenses. We wish to leave here in peace, and we will only fire if fired upon. However, if your attacks continue, any ship that fires upon us will be destroyed."

She waited for a reply.

None came; instead, Evans reported, "They're not answering us directly, Captain, but I'm picking up intership transmissions among the Hachai, ordering them not to listen to us, to destroy us at any cost."

She should have known they were too stubborn to give in so easily, Janeway told herself.

"Close the channel, Mr. Evans," she said. "Mr. Tuvok, fire on any ship that attacks us."

"I doubt very much that we will be able to carry out your threat, Captain," Tuvok said.

"I know that," Janeway replied. "Try to convince the Hachai we meant it, though."

"Firing phasers." An instant later, he added, "Reversing polarity."

"Mr. Paris," Janeway said, "get us out of here, however you can."

"I'm trying, Captain," Paris replied. "Believe me, I'm trying."

Janeway nodded, and tapped her combadge. "Janeway to Torres," she said.

"Torres here," came the reply.

"B'Elanna, if you've got anything extra left in those engines, make sure it's where Tom Paris can use it to get us out of here!"

"But what about Chako—"

Torres cut her protest short, biting it off in midname, before Janeway could do it for her.

"Yes, Captain," she said. "I'll see what I can do."

CHAPTER
21

WHATEVER P'NIR SHIP DESIGNERS HAD BEEN RESPONSI-
ble for the layout of this particular cruiser were not
given to wasting space on unnecessary corridors,
Harry Kim decided after he had doubled back for
the third or fourth time. Several passages that had
looked as if they ought to go through had dead-
ended, instead, and his idea of finding an alternate
route was beginning to look pretty stupid, in retrospect. He wondered if those P'nir workers, or
whoever they were, were still back there in the
main passage.

At least, he thought, he hadn't come across any
further signs of life as he made his way through the
side passages—there were no tapping feet or click-

ing claws to be heard anywhere, and he hadn't seen anything moving. He hadn't seen much of anything, what with the dim light and black walls— he'd had to go down corridors almost to the end to be sure they were dead ends.

The smell was just about the same here as everywhere else, a nasty oily smell, but he didn't think that meant anyone had been in the area; he was fairly sure the odor was a part of the atmosphere, and not something that came from the P'nir themselves.

For all he knew, it was their equivalent of air freshener, a little touch of home.

Aside from the silence, the already-dim greenish light seemed even dimmer here in this section, as if it were half-power emergency lighting; he'd gotten pretty confident that he wasn't going to meet anyone in this area. He wasn't sure what this part of the ship was really intended for, but it didn't seem to be in use just now.

He was thinking that when he rounded another corner and abruptly came face-to- . . . well, face-to-thorax with a P'nir. Kim's nose was no more than a meter from the hard, darkly gleaming surface of its exoskeleton.

This was his first look at one, and it was a bit startling. He'd guessed from the ship's architecture that they were tall and thin, but that hadn't prepared him for the reality. The P'nir was *very* tall, easily three meters or more—almost twice Kim's height. That blank face and the four red eyes seemed to be impossibly far above him.

Kim knew what he had to do. As he brought up his phaser and fired, he berated himself for having grown careless after seeing so many empty corridors; he hadn't been paying attention and had almost walked into this fellow.

The phaser's beam was intensely, painfully bright in the greenish gloom of what the P'nir apparently considered reasonable illumination.

Fortunately, the P'nir had been just as startled by the encounter as Kim, if not more so; after all, Kim had known there were hundreds of P'nir aboard, while the P'nir had had no idea that there were any humans running around loose. The P'nir didn't attack, or turn to flee, or do anything else that might have constituted a danger; instead it merely flailed about in a rather vague manner as Kim realized that his first shot had missed any crucial nerve junctions. He had dazed the P'nir, rather than rendering it unconscious. He fired again, aiming directly at its head.

It ignored that, and started reaching for him, now apparently over its initial astonishment. Kim saw that not only did the P'nir have complex and very fierce-looking claws, but the inner surfaces of the P'nir's upper arms were hard, serrated edges that looked distressingly sharp.

And since it was still conscious, Kim realized that the P'nir apparently didn't keep their brains in their heads, and he was too close to the P'nir to use a wide beam to hit the whole creature at once. Instead he ducked, to avoid those nasty cutting arms, then held the trigger button down and began waving the phaser back and forth, working his way down the P'nir's lengthy anatomy.

He had gotten the beam roughly halfway from the creature's head to its feet when the P'nir staggered, made an unhappy noise, and finally toppled over, to lean against the black corridor wall. It was too tall and rigid to fall all the way over in the confined space, and it had lodged with its head at an upward angle so that Kim couldn't see whether its eyes were open or closed, but it was clearly unconscious.

Harry straightened up, looked both ways along the corridor, and saw no sign that anyone else had seen or heard the incident. He looked down at the readouts on his phaser.

The charge level had dropped alarmingly; hand phasers were not meant for spraying about like garden hoses, even when set on stun. If he ran into any more P'nir—as he almost certainly would, since this one would be recovering soon and would undoubtedly spread the alarm and get the security forces out patrolling the corridors—he would need to take them down more efficiently if he wanted to get away.

He supposed he could have killed the unconscious P'nir, which would have eliminated the problem of what it would do when it woke up, but that was hardly an appropriate thing for him to do when he was there as part of a diplomatic mission. For all he knew, Chakotay had talked his way past the P'nir's initial hostility and was even now discussing peace terms with the P'nir captain. If Kim killed an innocent crew member, that might ruin everything.

Besides, Kim really didn't want to hurt anyone. The P'nir hadn't meant him any harm; it had just been in the wrong place at the wrong time.

Kim told himself he would just need to be more careful, and to move quickly—maybe he could reach the shuttlecraft before this fellow woke up, and before anyone found it.

But if he ran into any more P'nir, he really would need to use his phaser more effectively next time.

Judging by just where the beam had been pointed when the P'nir finally dropped, Harry decided that they kept their brains in the lower thorax, just above the joint in their exoskeletons that let them swivel their upper bodies. That also appeared to be where the chitin, or whatever their hides were made of, was thickest; there appeared to be overlapping layers of the greenish-black stuff.

That made sense, but it wasn't very convenient. And the lump that Kim thought was probably the braincase was at the back, which meant back-shooting would be more effective than a frontal attack, but somehow, judging by how the first one had behaved, he didn't think he was going to get many chances to shoot P'nir in the back.

He grimaced, took another look along the passage, then left the stunned P'nir and began jogging in the direction that he very much hoped would bring him back to the hangar where the shuttle waited.

He had guessed right, finally; he made only one

more wrong turn before at last, ten minutes later, emerging into the hangar bay.

The shuttlecraft stood out vividly against the dark black-and-green walls. Two P'nir guards were standing beside the shuttle's closed hatch; they hadn't spotted him yet as he stood in the corridor entrance, his mostly black uniform blending with the black walls.

After a moment's hesitation, Kim reset his phaser for maximum stun, adjusted the range and angle, then gunned both the guards down, aiming at the height where he thought their brains were.

It worked, though not as quickly as he hoped; one of them was able to touch a device on its belt, and the other managed to draw a weapon before collapsing. Seconds later an eerie, earsplittingly loud chirping sound rang through the ship—an alarm, Kim was sure.

He dashed to the shuttle in a series of astonishing low-gravity leaps and got aboard as quickly as he could, then sealed the hatch behind him.

He could still hear the alarm, very faintly.

The higher artificial gravity of the shuttle felt odd at first after so long aboard the P'nir cruiser, and he had to squint until his eyes readjusted to normal light, but in moments he was at the controls, scanning the interior of the P'nir cruiser.

The sensors showed only three humanoid lifeforms besides himself aboard the P'nir ship, and indicated that all three were wearing combadges; those had to be Chakotay and the others, and all three of them were in a room by themselves—so much, Kim thought, for any high-level discussions of peace being in progress.

Furthermore, he doubted any conferences were planned. The room where his three shipmates were located was just one of several similar rooms along a corridor, a layout that resembled a line of holding cells much more than it resembled a conference area, and the sensors showed no data links there; Kim could not imagine anyone holding an important conference without computer access.

A quick scan of the forward area that Kim thought must be the bridge showed the P'nir crew going about their business, and an exterior scan showed that the battle was still continuing as furiously as ever.

It seemed pretty obvious that Chakotay's mission had failed, and that he and the others were prisoners. And in that case, the obvious thing for Kim to do was to get the three of them out, as quickly as he could.

Kim hurried to the transporter controls.

A moment later the transporter effect shimmered and flared, and Chakotay, Rollins, and Bereyt stood there, a bit startled—Harry hadn't used his combadge to warn them, for fear the P'nir might overhear.

Chakotay was the first to recover. "Good work, Mr. Kim," he said, as he stepped from the transporter and headed for the pilot's seat. "What's our situation?"

"One of the guards set off an alarm before I could stun him," Kim reported. "Besides the guards, I stunned one in a passage about sixty meters from here, so they'll know one of us was there. I'm sorry."

Chakotay nodded. "You did fine. You got here alive and got us out, and that's plenty. What's the condition of the shuttlecraft?"

"I haven't had time to check anything but the sensors and the transporter, sir," Kim replied. "Those seem to be working just fine. I don't think any of the P'nir ever came aboard at all; the hatch was still closed when I got here. And did you get a *look* at them, sir? I'm not sure they'd *fit* in here."

"I got a look at them, Mr. Kim," Chakotay said. "You may be right."

"Thanks for the rescue, Harry," Bereyt said.

"So we're back where we started," Rollins said, "with the four of us in the shuttle. So how do we get out of here and back to the *Voyager*?"

Chakotay looked around, hoping for inspiration. "We could transport someone to Engineering and sabotage the tractor beams," he said. "And we might be able to blast our way out of this hangar bay if we have to."

"But we'd have to find their engineering section and locate the right equipment to sabotage," Bereyt said, "and even then, we'd still be in the middle of the battle." She studied the sensor reports Kim had left on the display. "In fact, we're down in the thick of it now, nowhere near clear space." She frowned, then adjusted the sensor settings and checked the results. "And Commander," she added, "so is the *Voyager*."

Chakotay whirled, sprang from his seat, and leaned over Bereyt's shoulder.

"Damn," he said.

"They must have followed us in," Rollins said.

"More likely they came too close, waiting for us, and the battle grew up around them, the same as it did for us," Chakotay replied. "Look, you see?" He pointed at the screen, at the fixed-star readings the sensors used to determine relative location. "The entire battle has shifted in that direction. That round thing we wanted to get a better look at that was in the center is near the farther edge, now." He frowned. "For that matter, so are we—this ship is moving in that direction at a pretty good speed."

"What does that mean?" Bereyt asked.

"That means it's carrying us farther away from the *Voyager*," Chakotay replied. "We can't expect any help from the captain unless we can get ourselves clear."

"If we go out there now we won't last a minute," Rollins said. "A shuttle's shields aren't going to hold up against that sort of barrage."

"And how long is the *Voyager* going to last out there?" Kim asked.

"Bereyt?" Chakotay said.

"So far so good, Commander," the Bajoran replied. "The *Voyager* seems to be holding her own. I can't get any exact readings from here, through the P'nir hull and the battle noise, but her shields are still there and she's still maneuvering freely."

Kim leaned over and watched.

"Looks to me like Tom Paris is at the helm," he said. "No one else we have can fly like that."

"I can," Chakotay said, his tone flat. Kim glanced up at the first officer's grim face, and remembered the problematic relationship between Paris and the first officer.

"Sorry, sir," Kim said, "I didn't mean . . ."

"Never mind," Chakotay said. "Just think of a way to get us safely out of here *and* out of the combat zone."

"It can't be done," Rollins said. He belatedly added, "Sir."

"As long as they're shooting at each other, there's a good chance we'd be hit by accident, even if they weren't shooting at *us,*" Kim said. "It'd be just about impossible to get safely through that firestorm out there."

" 'Just about'?" Chakotay asked.

"Well, they always told us, back at the Academy, that nothing is *completely* impossible," Kim said. "But I've got to say, sir, that I don't see any way out of here as long as the battle is going on out there."

Chakotay didn't look at Kim, but instead kept his eyes focused on the sensor displays as he said, "Well, then, we'll just have to do what Captain Janeway sent us here to do in the first place."

"Sir?"

"We'll just have to convince these people to *end* this battle!"

CHAPTER
22

TOM PARIS SENT THE *VOYAGER* INTO A SUDDEN SWOOP down and to port, then cut sharply up, dodging a concentrated burst of Hachai phased-energy beams; for an instant the *Voyager* was aimed directly at the stern assembly of a Hachai ship. Then, as two others brought their weapons to bear, Paris wheeled into a right-angle turn to port again, maneuvering the starship as if it were a fighter.

"Damn," he said, as he aimed for a gap between two dreadnaughts. "Tuvok, we had a perfect shot at that one; why didn't you take it?"

"I did not see it in time to use it effectively," the Vulcan replied. "My responses are no faster than a human's, and I was not able to anticipate the opportunity you provided. By the time I could have fired the aligning shot, and then reversed the polarity of the phasers, it would have been too late—we would have turned away."

"Tuvok, transfer the operation of our secondary phasers to conn," Janeway ordered, clutching the arms of her chair as the ship's artificial gravity wavered slightly under the combined assault of Hachai pounding and Tom Paris's piloting. "Set them to reverse polarity automatically after one second. Now, Mr. Paris, if you find another opportunity like that, you can take it yourself."

"Aye-aye," Paris acknowledged, as he flipped the ship around and wedged it through another opening in the Hachai formation. "If I can spare a finger."

"Secondary phaser control transferred, Captain," Tuvok said, "and I have already automated the polarity reversals." The primary phasers fired as he spoke, and after the usual interval of harmless dispersion, suddenly tore a gouge through a Hachai heat dissipation fin and cut deeply into a dreadnought's primary hull.

"Captain," Evans called from Operations, "I'm losing our fix on the P'nir cruiser that captured Commander Chakotay. It's moving off toward the far end of the battle, and there's too much interference, and too many identical ships, for me to keep track of it."

"Should I try to follow it, Captain?" Paris asked, never taking his hands off the controls or his eyes off the navigation screens.

The *Voyager* shuddered under another Hachai assault.

"No," Janeway said. "The *Voyager*'s safety is still our first priority. Just get us out of here, Mr. Paris, and we'll have to hope that Commander Chakotay can find his own way off that vessel."

"And if he can't . . ." Paris muttered, half to himself, as he swung the *Voyager* into another tight turn.

He didn't finish the sentence—and Janeway, overhearing the fragment, was glad of that.

Chakotay was Paris's protector from the animosity of the other Maquis, who saw Paris as a traitor.

He was also a rallying point for the Maquis, Janeway thought, and while he might take their side too often, Chakotay was also the best tool Janeway had for keeping the Maquis in line and integrating them into the crew.

Besides, his services as first officer were almost indispensable.

And quite outside any professional concerns, she liked and respected Chakotay; he was a good man, an honorable man. She did not want to abandon him—but the ship itself was her first responsibility. She not only had to get the ship out of the battle, she had to do it with as little damage as possible; there wasn't any starbase around the next sun where they could repair whatever the Hachai shot up.

"Damn," Paris said, as he veered the ship again, so sharply that the artificial gravity shifted a good twenty degrees for an instant. Something started to beep a warning, then went silent as Evans tended to it.

"What is it?" Janeway asked.

"A P'nir ship cut us off," Paris replied. "We were trying to squeeze through an opening in the Hachai englobement, and it cut in front of us."

"Then it was just trying to escape, the same as we are?" Janeway said. "It didn't fire on us?"

"No."

"Good," Janeway said emphatically. "We don't need another enemy out here, Mr. Paris."

"Captain, it's the P'nir who took Chakotay prisoner and got us into this mess," Paris replied. "I hardly think that's the act of . . ."

He broke off as he concentrated on a complicated maneuver, then finished, ". . . a *friend.*"

The ship shook as three smaller Hachai vessels passed it by, firing their weapons in what resembled a strafing run; Tuvok's phasers flashed out and tore a chunk of impulse engine off one of the three, sending it into a spin that brought it crashing against a Hachai dreadnought. Their shields saved both ships from a fiery end, but the force of the impact collapsed the smaller one into wreckage.

"Nice shot," Paris said. "Captain, we're almost out—once we get through that gap up to starboard, at bearing one three three mark six zero five, we'll be in open space."

"Thank you, Mr. Paris."

"I still think we should be shooting at the P'nir, as well as the Hachai," he said, as he swung the

Voyager around in a turn designed to make the Hachai think that he hadn't seen the opening and was heading the wrong way.

"Mr. Paris, the P'nir may not be our friends, but at least they are not shooting at *us*," Janeway told him. "I'd like to keep it that way."

"Aye-aye," Paris reluctantly acknowledged.

"Besides," Janeway pointed out, "we don't know how effective the P'nir shields are against us. We haven't analyzed their waveform patterns; they may not have the same susceptibility to our phasers that the Hachai technology has. And the P'nir *do* have our friends aboard one of their ships, Mr. Paris; if we start firing at the P'nir, Chakotay and the others may be killed in revenge."

Paris didn't answer her explanation in words, but Janeway thought his shoulders slumped slightly as the truth of her words sank in.

His hands didn't leave the controls, though, and the *Voyager* continued her planned feint and dash.

Janeway watched as the view on the main screen wheeled majestically, the immense array of warships sliding by as *Voyager* came around to head for the opening in the Hachai screen. The ships blocked out the stars, there were so many of them—the striped gray behemoths of the Hachai, the shadowy, jagged black of the P'nir, in one great shifting pattern that seemed to stretch on to infinity, all of it lit with the red and orange fire of energy weapons and the blue-green flaring of shields, shadowed with clouds of powdered wreckage.

And then they were turning away from the heart of the battle, and she could see the hard black of interstellar space, blacker than any P'nir hull and strewn with the sharp light of stars, between the moving ships. The screen of ships grew thinner, the holes between them wider, as *Voyager*'s nose swung around.

And there was the opening through which Paris intended to take them out, a space where there weren't enough Hachai ships to complete an englobement, where P'nir light cruisers had forced a dreadnought out of formation for a moment.

"B'Elanna, you'd better have the engines ready for me," Paris said, as the turn slowed and he reached for the warp drive controls.

Janeway tensed as she realized that Paris, who up until now had been maneuvering the ship entirely on thrusters or impulse, intended to slam on the warp drive, to send them out through that hole before the Hachai could close it.

If he missed, though, the ship's shields wouldn't save them; impact with a Hachai ship at warp speeds would reduce both ships to little more than a spray of gamma rays and superheated hydrogen.

And then, before Paris's hand hit the panel, a P'nir cruiser sailed into the opening.

"*Damn* it!" Paris shouted, and the hand that had been reaching for the warp drive instead slammed down onto the phaser trigger.

The secondary phasers flashed out.

"No!" Janeway shouted, rising from her chair. "Mr. Paris, I . . ."

Then she stopped in midsentence, fascinated by what she saw on the viewscreen.

The instant polarity reversed, the phasers went through the P'nir light cruiser's shields like a Klingon knife through fresh meat. The power drop from penetrating the defenses couldn't have been more than ten percent at the absolute most, Janeway judged, and the beam had hit the P'nir ship's main fuselage slightly aft of center.

It was a good, solid blow, but nothing that any Alpha Quadrant starship couldn't handle. The secondaries were less powerful than the *Voyager*'s primary armament, and the P'nir shields had cut their effectiveness slightly; furthermore, the hit hadn't been on anything particularly crucial, such as a main drive or magazine.

A Federation starship would have shuddered, maybe taken a few minor casualties as crewmen slammed into bulkheads or were struck by flying debris. The crew of a Klingon cruiser, with its heavier armor, wouldn't even have noticed the blow as some refractory coating burned away.

But the P'nir ship had virtually collapsed; several of the jutting, spiky protrusions had folded in on themselves or sheared off, while the main hull buckled. Atmosphere was boiling out from several ruptures.

Janeway shuddered at the thought of the slaughter they had just inflicted.

They got a good, close look at the damage as the *Voyager* sailed up near the crippled vessel, aiming for the opening in the Hachai formation—an opening that was no longer there. Three more P'nir light cruisers were blocking the *Voyager*'s path out to open space.

"Damn!" Paris said again, as he swung the ship about sharply, looking for another exit.

"Good try, Mr. Paris," Janeway said, "and we'll talk about shooting at the wrong side later. Meanwhile, see if you can find us another way out. Tuvok, analysis—what happened to that cruiser?"

"Fascinating," Tuvok replied, as he put a recorded image of the P'nir vessel's destruction on one of his wall screens and began playing through it in slow motion. Even as he did, however, he kept one hand on fire control, ready to retaliate against any attacker.

"It would seem, Captain," Tuvok said, "that the P'nir place such confidence in their shields, or perhaps were so short of metals, that they have used the energy fields of the shields themselves as structural members in the construction of their ships—the fields form a sort of exoskeleton that not only protects the ship, but supports it. The integrity of the hull *without* the shields would appear to be insufficient to withstand even the normal stresses of interstellar travel, let alone the impact of a Type Four phaser."

Just then the ship shook; the main viewer blanked out, and the blue-white glare of overloaded shields lit the bridge. The feedback rumbled through the ship, drowning out the sound of the *Voyager*'s own phasers returning fire. Janeway grabbed the forward console for support.

"More Hachai?" she asked.

"No," Paris said, as he threw the ship into another turn, "I managed to dodge the Hachai that time. That was the P'nir who hit us."

"Damn," Janeway said.

"The P'nir are now concentrating fire on us," Tuvok reported. "However, the Hachai appear to be breaking off their attack in confusion."

"I don't care *who* we're fighting," Janeway snapped. "Take us *out* of here, Mr. Paris!"

"I'm trying, Captain, believe me!"

"Mr. Paris, if the Hachai are no longer firing at us . . ." Janeway said.

She didn't need to finish the sentence. "Right, Captain," Paris replied. "I'll try to go through them." He swung the ship into yet another jarring turn.

Janeway watched the battle on the screens. The P'nir in this area had not originally intended to fight the *Voyager;* they were there to harass the Hachai and to take advantage of any damage the stranger did to their ancient enemy. Half a dozen light cruisers had been weaving through the formations of Hachai dreadnoughts, not so much fighting anyone as merely annoying their enemies. One of them had cut off the *Voyager*'s escape, apparently in hopes of keeping the strange ship trapped where it would do more damage to the Hachai.

No one out there seemed to have expected the *Voyager* to damage the P'nir.

When the *Voyager* crippled the P'nir cruiser and the sides suddenly changed, the P'nir ships in the vicinity had all immediately opened fire on the *Voyager,* but they were in no position for any sort of entrapping maneuvers, and they had no real defenses to protect them against the *Voyager's* counterattacks.

They had no defenses except their shields.

For decades, those shields had been enough to protect the P'nir.

Now, however, the *Voyager's* phasers were ripping through those shields at will, destroying the fields that held the P'nir warcraft together, crippling ship after ship—but other P'nir ships were coming in behind them, forcing their way through the suddenly porous Hachai lines. Turning and dodging was no longer the *Voyager's* best strategy; the P'nir were all behind them, and charging forward en masse, in such numbers that the *Voyager* would almost certainly be utterly destroyed before it could knock them all out of action.

The only sensible strategy was to run.

The only problem was that ahead of them, between the *Voyager* and the freedom and safety of empty space, were the remains of a Hachai englobement force.

The Hachai were no longer laying down fields of fire or interlocking their shields, no longer linking their isolated ships into a solid wall of destructive energy, but escape would still mean passing directly between two of the immense Hachai dreadnoughts, with no more than a kilometer or so of clearance on either side.

A kilometer was a goodly distance on a planetary

surface, but out here in space it was almost nothing. If Paris, at the helm, were to misjudge the angle, they might well collide with one of the dreadnoughts. Or if the Hachai opened fire at that range . . .

And then Paris hit the warp drive controls, and Janeway didn't have any more time to worry about it as the scarred gray surfaces of the Hachai ships swept toward them at impossible speed.

CHAPTER
23

"YOU HEARD WHAT THE STRIPED ONE SAID BACK THERE in our cell," Chakotay said. "It matches what Neelix told us. The P'nir give their captains immense authority and freedom to act on their own. We need to talk to the captain if we want to get anywhere!"

"But the captain doesn't seem to want to talk to us," Rollins said.

"Um, Commander," Kim said, "I think . . . well, there are a lot of P'nir outside right now. I think they've figured out that we're back aboard here." He pointed.

Chakotay looked. As Kim had said, there were dozens of P'nir in the hangar, formed up in three lines, all of them pointing their hand weapons in the general direction of the shuttlecraft.

"Move us over by the main door," Chakotay ordered. "If they blast us with enough to puncture our hull, it'll go through *their* hull, as well. They won't like that."

"Yes, sir," Kim said. He threw power to the shuttle's lifters, and a moment later the little craft bumped gently against the solidly closed portal.

The P'nir guards watched, then milled about in confusion, looking about for orders.

Kim turned from the controls and said, "If we can't get to the captain, what if we were to bring the captain here?"

Chakotay snapped his head around to stare at him for a fraction of a second; then he nodded.

"Good," he said. "Very good. We can't get a lock on her blind, though—"

"I'll go," Kim said. "Give me an extra combadge; I'll tag her with it, and you can get a fix on that."

"Good," Chakotay repeated. "Bereyt, scan the ship for us and find some likely coordinates. Rollins, you'll work the transporter. . . ."

A moment later Ensign Kim flashed into existence in the center of the P'nir cruiser's bridge.

The bridge was a wedge-shaped space fifteen meters long, its sloping floor highest at the point and a good two meters lower at the curve. Workstations lined the curve, with an immense viewscreen above them, all in clear view of the one green-painted P'nir who slumped comfortably, arms draped over metal bars, up near the point.

That one P'nir was obviously the captain; the paint covered almost its entire torso, and Kim considered this confirmation that body-paint must be, as they had earlier surmised, a sign of high rank.

Even as Kim realized that, the captain screamed, making a high-pitched hissing, whistling noise like a steam boiler about to explode. Several of the dozen P'nir at the workstations started to turn.

"Security! You missed one! It's here!" the captain shrieked.

Before any of the P'nir could react, Kim ran up the slope and slapped the combadge in his hand against the P'nir captain's thorax. He simultaneously slapped his own combadge with his other hand.

"Energize!" he said.

The world seemed to freeze, then shimmer, and then he and the captain were aboard the shuttle. Chakotay stood before them, phaser in hand.

The P'nir captain attempted to straighten from her comfortable crouch and immediately whacked her head hard against the roof of the shuttlecraft— she had arrived with no more than a centimeter's clearance.

The P'nir ducked again and looked about—Kim wasn't sure whether she was astonished, angry, confused, or what.

Chakotay pointed the phaser up at the P'nir's face.

"Now, Captain," he said calmly, "you *will* negotiate with me!"

The P'nir captain screamed again, as it had back on the bridge; Rollins and Kim winced, and Bereyt clapped her hands over her ears. It tried to straighten up again, hit its head again, and resumed its crouch—the shuttle's interior simply wasn't designed for anything as tall as a P'nir.

But then, still crouching, the P'nir charged at Chakotay, its claws spread wide and its serrated arm-parts raised ready to slice.

Chakotay fired his phaser at the alien captain's head, and then ducked quickly under the vicious swipe of one cutting edge as the stun-beam failed to stop the furious creature.

"Aim for the middle, Commander!" Kim shouted. "Just above the swivel-joint!"

Chakotay fired again, and the P'nir tottered, slumped, and then fell heavily to one side, to lean awkwardly against a bulkhead.

"I hope she didn't crack her exoskeleton," Bereyt said, hurrying to the downed P'nir's side.

Chakotay, once he was sure the P'nir was unconscious, didn't waste any time on such niceties; he turned and said, "I wish you'd told me that sooner, Mr. Kim. Mr. Rollins, give me exterior audio."

"Yes, sir."

A second later the occupants of the shuttle heard the clicking and rattling of a few dozen P'nir moving about; voices murmured quietly, the words indistinguishable. Then a command came from somewhere, plainly audible.

"Destroy the alien craft!" a P'nir voice ordered.

"Shields up, Mr. Rollins," Chakotay snapped.

"But we're still next to the hangar door . . ." Rollins protested, even as he activated the shields.

"Some of them may not remember that in time," Chakotay said. "Or maybe they've decided that the hangar door is more solid than it looks. Mr. Kim, open a channel to the P'nir bridge—or if they refuse contact, just give me exterior speakers."

"They're evacuating the hangar, sir," Rollins reported. "Maybe they're willing to blow out the door to get us, after all."

"Keep those shields up," Chakotay ordered. "If they *do* blow out the door, at least we'll be able to get off their confounded ship."

In the stern area, Bereyt had lowered the P'nir captain to the deck and inspected her for injuries, but had found none. Now she looked up from where she knelt by the still-unconscious creature and said, "But they could still tractor us back in, if that happens."

"More likely they'd just blow us to bits," Chakotay said. "No point in making it easy for them."

"They're refusing contact, sir, but I've got the exterior speakers, and there's still air in the hangar," Kim reported. "They should be able to hear you."

"This is Commander Chakotay, of the Federation starship *Voyager*," Chakotay announced. "We have your captain in here with us, alive and well; if you destroy us, you'll destroy her, as well."

He waited, but no one answered at first.

The eventual reply was not directed at the shuttle, but at the P'nir crew.

"Mourn, O P'nir," a voice commanded. "The aliens have taken K't'rien from us! Obey me, Tsh'pak, as your captain now, and destroy every trace of the aliens, expunge them from existence!"

For a moment, the four in the shuttlecraft looked at one another in silence.

"They still don't seem to be interested in negotiating," Kim said wryly.

"You know, Commander," Rollins said, "that voice sounds familiar. It might be the striped one who visited us in our cell."

"Or it might not," Chakotay said. "We don't know how much their voices vary."

"What does it matter if it *is* the same one you talked to?" Kim asked.

"That one might have something of a grudge against us," Chakotay explained. "We weren't very cooperative when it tried to interrogate us."

"Commander," Bereyt asked from where she knelt beside the unconscious P'nir, "do you think it might be just this one person who's responsible for their refusal to talk? Maybe the captain still has loyalists, and if we could reach them, or remove this one officer . . ."

"What do you mean?"

"I mean we could transport this Tsh'pak aboard, just as we did their captain . . ." Bereyt began.

"We'd have to drop the shields," Chakotay snapped. "I don't think that's a good idea right now."

The shuttle's hull suddenly rang, as if struck by something heavy.

"They're firing at us," Rollins reported. "Just small arms; the shields are handling it just fine."

"Where are they firing *from?*" Chakotay asked, striding up to look over Rollins's shoulder at the external video display. "Didn't they evacuate the hangar?"

"Yes, they did," Rollins said, "but they're back."

"So they are," Chakotay said.

A dozen or so P'nir had reentered the hangar, wearing clear helmets that covered their heads and shoulders, as well as gloves, boots, and belts—presumably their equivalent of spacesuits; the exoskeletons would make full-body coverage unnecessary.

Each of these P'nir held a weapon that looked like an unholy hybrid of rifle and octopus—weapons they were firing at the shuttle.

Chakotay stared for a moment, then turned away. "You saw the setup on the bridge," he said to Kim. "Do you think it's just one power-hungry second-in-command? Or is this a cultural thing, that they abandon hostages?"

Kim hesitated.

"I don't know, sir," he said at last. "Their command arrangements appear very authoritarian—the captain literally looks down on all the others, and none of them can see her face without turning around. But I don't know what that would mean about how they deal with successions or hostage situations."

"You heard Bereyt's suggestion; do you think we should kidnap the new captain, too?" Chakotay asked.

"I think it's worth trying," Bereyt said, before Kim could reply.

"Sir," Kim pointed out, as the hull rang again beneath another barrage, "we can't drop the shields safely while they're firing at us, and we can't use the transporter while the shields are up."

"They can't fire at us forever," Rollins said.

"Our shields won't hold forever, either," Chakotay replied. "And I don't particularly want to spend the rest of my life here."

"Commander," Bereyt called, from back toward the stern, "she's coming around."

Chakotay saw that the P'nir captain's hands were waving feebly. The red slit-eyes had never closed— there didn't appear to be any lids or nictitating membranes, so they *couldn't* close—but they had appeared dim and fogged, and now seemed to be brightening again.

"Kim, Bereyt, hold her limbs," Chakotay snapped. He lifted his phaser, checked the setting, and leveled it at the P'nir's midsection.

The P'nir turned her head to look at him.

"Captain," he said, "welcome aboard my ship."

She looked at him, her featureless face unreadable, then demanded, "Tell me why I still live."

"Because we want to talk to you," Chakotay said. "That's all we ever wanted. We want to know why your people are fighting the Hachai, and whether there's anything we can do to stop the war."

The P'nir stared at him, and didn't speak.

"Tell me why you're fighting the Hachai," Chakotay said, remembering the need to use imperatives.

"To destroy them," the P'nir replied.

"Ah," Chakotay said. "And tell me why you wish to destroy them."

"Because they are . . ." She hesitated, as if groping for the right words. "They are unfit. They are repulsive."

"By which you mean they're not P'nir," Bereyt said, with disgust plain in her voice. "I've heard this before, Commander, from the Cardassians."

Chakotay nodded. "You may be right," he said. "Plenty of cultures go through a stage of thinking they're right and anyone different is wrong." He turned back to the P'nir. "Then you won't consider peace with the Hachai?" He added belatedly, "Tell me the truth."

"There is no reason to consider peace," the P'nir captain replied.

"If you continue to fight, thousands of P'nir will die in the conflict," Chakotay pointed out.

The P'nir didn't seem to be troubled by that; she didn't answer.

"Tell me whether you think your second-in-command would agree with you that there is no reason to consider peace," Chakotay said.

"I have no command," the P'nir said bitterly.

Chakotay snapped his head up and stared at Kim, who spread his hands in incomprehension. "She *has* to be the captain, sir," he said. "She was in the obvious position of command on the bridge. And didn't they announce that the captain was gone?"

"Tell us what you mean," Chakotay said, pointing the phaser at the P'nir. "Aren't you the captain of this cruiser? What was the name . . . K't'rien? Aren't you K't'rien?"

"I am K't'rien," the P'nir agreed, "but I am captain no more. I am disgraced. I have acted improperly; I left the bridge in time of combat."

"You were *taken* from the bridge, against your will," Chakotay corrected her.

"That is worse."

"And what if we took this Tsh'pak, who has replaced you, from the bridge?" Chakotay asked.

"Then she, too, would be disgraced and unable to command," the P'nir said.

Chakotay frowned. "And then someone else would take her place?"

"F'shrin would be next," K't'rien confirmed.

"So much for that idea," Rollins said. "We can't keep kidnapping them until the whole crew's in here."

"If we released you, put you back on the bridge, would you be the captain again?" Bereyt asked.

When the P'nir didn't reply, Chakotay raised the phaser and ordered, "Answer her."

"I must defeat my captors, unaided, and return to the bridge unaided, to remove the disgrace and be restored to propriety," the P'nir said. "Even then, any who chose might challenge me to show that I had acted properly and had not yielded incorrectly to anyone. If you released me and you still resisted, I would be marked a traitor and destroyed."

"Vicious," Bereyt said.

"That's a worse attitude than even the hard-line Klingons have," Kim added.

"If you release me and then flee, I can claim to have defeated you and escaped," the P'nir said, her voice suddenly calmer. "I may say that I spared your lives and ship so that we could recapture you for later study, so that we might learn how you took me from the bridge."

Chakotay stared at her, considering that.

Behind him, at the shuttle's controls, Rollins glanced at the viewscreen showing the hangar, then cleared his throat. "Sir," he said, "I think you should take a look at this. Right now. Because whatever you decide to do, I think you'd better do it quickly."

CHAPTER
24

FOR AN INSTANT, JANEWAY HAD A CLOSER LOOK AT THE hull of a Hachai dreadnought than she had ever wanted—the image on the viewscreen showed her every detail, every rivet, every scar accumulated in hundreds of years of combat.

Then the *Voyager* was past the dreadnought and out in relatively open space again, amid the empty blackness and the cold light of distant stars—though they were still inside the cloud of metal dust and freeze-dried blood that surrounded the battle.

Yet they were, at least for the moment, free, and the ship was more or less intact.

"Status report," she ordered, turning. "Mr. Tuvok!"

"We are clear of the main area of battle," the Vulcan replied. "However, several P'nir ships appear to be attempting pursuit, and the Hachai seem to be undecided as to whether or not to impede the P'nir in this. Certain Hachai vessels are moving to block the P'nir, while others appear to be deliberately making way for them."

Janeway nodded, and turned back to face forward again. "Mr. Paris?"

"As Tuvok said, we're out of the battle zone," Paris replied, "and *Voyager* can outrun anything the P'nir have, if that's what you want to do. At the moment we're on a heading of one-three-one mark eight, at warp five—not heading much of anywhere, but getting there fast."

Janeway looked up. "Engineering!"

"We're fine down here, Captain," B'Elanna Torres replied. "The shields held up beautifully and kept anyone from doing any real damage—I've got a few bruised crew members, a cracked instrument panel, and some blown-out power conduits—we did get knocked around a little—but there's nothing seriously wrong here. There's nothing we can't fix once we've got a few hours to spare. We've used up all our reserve power, but we can rebuild that any time you're willing to stay at less than warp speeds for a while."

"Sickbay—what's the situation there?"

For a moment no one replied, and Janeway feared the worst; then Neelix said, "We're fine here, Captain—at least, I am, and Kes is, and I suppose the doctor is, if it really makes any difference for a hologram. We're pretty busy right now, though—the doctor and Kes are too busy to talk."

"What about the casualties?" Janeway demanded.

"Well, no one's been killed," the Talaxian reported thoughtfully, "but we certainly do have a lot of burns and bumps and bruises. One crewman cracked his skull against a bulkhead a few minutes ago, and the doctor's working on him right now, while Kes tends the burn patients."

"Thank you, Mr. Neelix," Janeway said, greatly relieved to know that no one had died. Then she turned left, to Ops. "Mr. Evans," she said, "any sign of our shuttlecraft?"

"I'm afraid not, Captain. But at this distance, and this speed . . ."

Janeway didn't wait for him to finish the sentence; she turned and snapped, "Mr. Paris, drop to impulse. Then turn this ship around and take us back."

"Back into the battle, Captain?" Paris protested.

"No," Janeway said. "Just close enough to be ready when Chakotay comes out looking for us."

Paris blinked. "You think he will?"

"I intend to at least give him a chance, Mr. Paris!" Janeway replied.

CHAPTER
25

IT WASN'T HARD TO SEE WHY ROLLINS HAD THOUGHT something needed to be done quickly. Chakotay stared over Rollins's shoulder at the image on the display.

A dozen P'nir were hauling machinery into the hangar, fitting components together, and making adjustments to the resulting assembly.

"What *is* that they're building?" he asked.

"I don't know, sir," Kim replied, "but whatever it is, that appears to be an energy projector of some sort on this side of it."

Chakotay looked at the elaborate machinery out in the hangar for another second, then turned to the disgraced captain. "Tell me what they're doing," he said.

"No," she replied. "Surrender to me, restore me to my place!"

Chakotay turned away in disgust.

"Sir," Kim said, "I notice that they've stopped shooting at us."

"They've probably given up," Rollins said. "They must have figured out they can't get through our shields with hand weapons."

"Exactly," Kim agreed. "They can't get us with hand weapons—but I don't think they've given up. The P'nir don't seem to give up easily."

"What are you talking about?" Rollins asked.

Kim pointed at the screen. "My guess would be that that thing they're putting together is something that *can* punch through our shields. It might be a weapon they moved in here from somewhere else, or maybe it's some sort of construction equipment . . ."

"You're right," Chakotay said, looking at the thing. Now that the assembly was largely complete and most of the workers had cleared away, he could see more of the machine. A central coil amid a tangle of modulators was mounted on a box that was presumably a power regulator, and the coil fed into a parabolic projection dish; the technology wasn't quite like anything he'd seen before, but the basic principles behind its construction seemed clear enough.

"They plan to batter down our shields and kill us all, I'd say," Chakotay said.

"Do you think it'll work, sir?" Kim asked.

"It should," Chakotay replied.

"We have to stop them!" Rollins blurted.

"What did you have in mind?" Chakotay asked. "We can't use the shuttle's phasers in here. . . ."

"We could go out with hand phasers . . ." Kim began, then stopped.

Chakotay considered that for a moment, picturing it; the image of the four of them bursting out the shuttle hatch and blasting the P'nir energy projector reminded him of something, but it took a second before he could recover and identify the memory.

A sally, he realized, as in medieval European warfare. Like knights venturing out of a besieged fortress to destroy a catapult or siege tower.

That image exactly paralleled the situation they were in—a besieged castle, with the outnumbered defenders hiding behind their walls while the enemy brought up whatever machinery was necessary to break in.

In such a case, a sally might drive back the attackers, destroy the siege machinery . . . but it wouldn't change the inevitable outcome.

Chakotay had studied military history and theory of warfare at the Academy; he knew that the only way defenders *ever* won a properly conducted siege was if some outside force came to their rescue. The point of the defense was to stay alive until one's allies could attack the besieging force from the rear. A sally wouldn't decide anything by itself; it was merely a delaying tactic, a move to delay the inevitable and give one's allies more time to arrive.

Chakotay realized, however, that his allies were not coming. Oh, he didn't doubt that Janeway would *want* to rescue him, but he didn't believe she *could,* not while they were trapped deep inside the ongoing battle. . . .

"Mr. Rollins," he said, "run a scan of the battle. I want to know where we are, and where the *Voyager* is."

"Yes, sir." As Rollins went to work, Chakotay began reviewing his options.

He could surrender, as K't'rien asked—but she had not actually said that they would be set free again if they did surrender, and even if she had, he had no reason to believe P'nir promises. The Hachai certainly put no faith in them.

The defenders of a besieged castle who surrendered were completely at the mercy of the victors; there were plenty of examples in history of both mercy and ruthless slaughter, and of victorious besiegers breaking their promises.

The four of them could hold out here for as long as possible, in hopes that Janeway and the *Voyager* would come to their rescue—but it was a thin hope, at best. The P'nir cruiser was a purpose-built warship at least ten times the *Voyager*'s size, and with a thousand allies close at hand; even if Janeway was foolish enough to try it, her chances of succeeding, despite the slight technological edge, were slim.

They could make the sally that Ensign Kim had suggested, to destroy the energy projector, but that would only prolong the siege, not end it.

There was one other possibility . . . escape. Many castles were built with secret tunnels that let the defenders escape a siege, and the shuttlecraft's transporter filled that role nicely.

But if the four of them escaped—five, with K't'rien—where would they go? What would they do? They had no realistic chance of taking over a ship this size and forcing it to take them safely back to the *Voyager,* not when the P'nir reaction to a hostage captain was to consider the hostage disgraced and worthless.

They could use the transporter "tunnel" to send their forces behind the enemy lines and wreak havoc—that, too, was a traditional, if risky, maneuver in siege warfare—but Chakotay did not see how that would get them safely off this ship and out of the battle. . . .

"Commander!" Rollins called. "I think you'd better see this."

Chakotay leaned over the ensign's shoulder and looked at the displays again.

Rollins had not been looking at the exterior video of the hangar this time; he had been running sensor scans of the battle outside. The details were hazy, since the scanners had to work through the P'nir hull and two sets of shields, but a few facts were clear immediately.

The cruiser on which they were held had moved, had worked its way through the battle zone almost from end to end, and if it didn't change course soon, they were about to emerge from one end of the cloud of warships, out into open space.

The distraction of the captain's kidnapping was probably partly responsible for that, Chakotay guessed; this ship would not be in top fighting form while its officers and crew were busy with the invader in their hangar bay and the transition of power to the new captain. The ship was still fighting, but it was being moved into a less-crucial outer position.

While that maneuver lasted the shuttle would have the best chance of escaping into clear space that they could possibly hope for. It still wouldn't be an easy ride, by any means, but they'd have a chance, especially if the *Voyager* was nearby and spotted them in time. If they could once get the shuttlecraft off the P'nir cruiser . . .

Another interesting fact to be read from the display was their location relative to the huge spheroid that had attracted Janeway's attention almost as soon as they saw the battle, the great round object that was plainly neither Hachai nor P'nir, the thing that had emitted strange radiation, including tetryon radiation, that they had hoped might have meant it had some connection with the Caretaker's lost companion.

They were passing quite near the mysterious object; the battle had shifted so that it was no longer at the center, but instead near one end. And they, aboard the P'nir ship, were between the stranger and the edge of the combat area, about to emerge into empty space.

That meant that the mysterious object would

shield them from much of the battle, making this an even better opportunity to escape.

And it meant more than that . . .

"Give me a close-up on that thing," Chakotay said.

Rollins tapped the controls, and Chakotay studied the results. There was no direct visual of the object, but the shuttle computers were able to construct an image from the energy readings—an image of a gigantic, almost spherical construct, its surface divided into cell-like structures.

Some of those cells were missing, and a dozen holes gaped in the thing's sides, holes big enough to swallow a Galaxy-class starship.

"I've seen something like that before," Chakotay said. His recent mental review of what the Academy had taught him about siege warfare had him in the right frame of mind for recovering half-forgotten old lessons.

"Sir, it's a derelict . . ." Rollins said.

"It's huge," Kim added.

"History tapes," Chakotay said. "At the Academy. I remember a ship like that."

"You're right, sir," Kim said. "From . . . eighty years ago, I think it was."

"The First Federation," Chakotay said. "That was what they called themselves. The captain that met their ship sent one of his crew as an ambassador, and then we never heard anything more from them."

"James Kirk, on the *Enterprise*," Kim agreed. "He bluffed them with some nonsense about a super-explosive, and then found out that they'd been bluffing, too. We covered it in Strategy and Tactics, second year."

"Looks like they ran into the Hachai and the P'nir and found out they *weren't* bluffing," Rollins said.

"Or maybe it was just drifting, already wrecked, and the P'nir and the Hachai found it," Chakotay said. "It doesn't really matter how it got here; what matters is that it's not the Caretaker's companion, and there's nothing there that's going to help us get home."

"Do we know that, sir?" Kim asked. "If the First Federation contacted *our* Federation eighty years ago. . . ."

Chakotay shook his head. "Take another look." He reached down and tapped a control, and the image zoomed in.

"It's hollow!" Rollins exclaimed.

Kim nodded, remembering. "That's right," he said. "That was the bluff—the big ship wasn't much more than an empty shell. The *real* ship was incredibly powerful, but it was relatively tiny."

"And the real ship, as well as anything else worthwhile, is gone," Chakotay said. He pointed. "Look."

The others looked, and saw that P'nir ships were maneuvering *through* the First Federation derelict, dodging in and out of the holes in its side to harass the Hachai, and the Hachai were shooting into the openings after them.

"They wouldn't be doing that if there was anything of any possible value left in there," Kim agreed. "The emissions must just be residual—secondary radiation."

Chakotay nodded. "Or maybe something on there still worked well enough to put out that tetryon beam." He pointed at a sensor readout.

One cell on the derelict's hull was producing faint and fading secondary tetryon emissions.

"It's worthless," Rollins said bitterly. "This was all for nothing!"

"It was an attempt at peacemaking, Ensign," Chakotay said. "That's always worth trying."

"Well, it didn't work," Rollins said.

"No, it didn't," Chakotay agreed. "But it was worth the try. And now that we know it didn't work, all we need to do is get *out* of here!"

"How?" Rollins demanded.

"Well, I could take a few shots at that projector, or whatever it is, with my phaser," Kim said. "That'll buy us some time."

"We need to take out the tractor beam, open the hangar door, and get clear before the P'nir can blow us to dust," Chakotay said. "Do we know how to do that?" He turned to look at the Bajoran.

"No," Bereyt said. "I've scanned the ship as best I can, but I couldn't make much sense of it. Their design isn't like anything I'm familiar with. I found the bridge, and the storerooms, but beyond that . . . well, I'm not even sure where Engineering is."

"But we have someone who could tell us what we need to know," Chakotay said, jerking his chin at their P'nir captive. "All we have to do is convince her."

The others looked at him nervously; Bereyt glanced back at the P'nir, then back at him.

She was probably remembering Cardassian methods for "convincing" prisoners to cooperate, Chakotay realized. And she was probably wondering just how many of the stories circulating in Starfleet about ruthless Maquis terrorists were based on truth.

And judging by Rollins's expression, he had believed those stories about the Maquis all along. Harry Kim was the only one who didn't seem to expect Chakotay to start breaking open the P'nir's claws and yanking out the marrow.

"I don't know how we can do that, sir," he said. "What can we offer her?"

"We can offer her her position as captain back," Chakotay replied. He turned to face the P'nir.

"Listen, K't'rien," he said, "we can arrange for you to 'escape' once you've shown us what we need to shut down to get us out of here safely."

The P'nir stared at him silently.

"You can defeat us, and we'll flee," Chakotay said. "At least, that's what it'll look like. We'll be gone, and you'll be able to reassert yourself as captain. We all win. But you'll have to show us how to shut down the tractor beam and open the hangar door, and swear to do what you can to give us a few seconds to get clear before this ship opens fire."

"Commander," Kim whispered urgently, "not to

impugn anyone's honor, but . . . well, do we really know what the P'nir attitude toward swearing and keeping oaths is? Particularly oaths made to non-P'nir?"

"It's a calculated risk, Ensign," Chakotay whispered back. "They taught you about those at the Academy, didn't they? And we need to act *now,* before this ship's crew reorganizes and dives back into the thick of the fray."

"Yes, sir." Kim fell silent, and Chakotay turned back to the P'nir.

K't'rien stared at Chakotay, her red eyes gleaming. She didn't speak.

"K't'rien, give me your promise to aid us," Chakotay said. "When we have your sworn oath, we will release you and we will flee."

For a long moment the P'nir didn't reply; then, abruptly, she said, "Tell me what aid you require."

"We need to know how to disable your ship's tractor beam—only temporarily—and open the hangar door so that our craft can leave," Chakotay explained.

"That is all?"

"That is all."

The P'nir seemed to consider for a moment—though with her featureless face it was hard to be sure what, if anything, she might be thinking. "Confirm or deny this," she said at last. "You propose to listen to my instruction, then hold me here while you carry it out."

"Well, yes, that's what we had in mind," Chakotay said warily.

"I refuse to cooperate with that proposal," the P'nir immediately replied. "I cannot trust you to do no other damage to the ship that was once mine."

"Then propose an alternative," Chakotay said. The P'nir style of speaking without questions was beginning to come naturally for him.

"I will disable the tractor beam and open the door," K't'rien replied. "I will not instruct you, but I will do it myself."

"You expect us to trust you?" Chakotay asked. "To release you?"

K't'rien didn't answer. Chakotay frowned. Of course she didn't answer, he told himself; he'd asked her a question instead of giving her an order.

"Commander," Kim said, "What if I went with her? You could keep a transporter fix on us. . . ."

"We can't risk keeping the shuttle's shields down that long," Chakotay objected. "We couldn't maintain a transporter lock."

"Well, we'll have combadges," Kim said, "or at least, I'll have mine, and I can call for help. It shouldn't take more than a few seconds to drop the shields, lock on, and retrieve us."

Chakotay considered that. He didn't like it—but he didn't see a better alternative.

"Do it," he said.

CHAPTER
26

THE BIG PROJECTOR THAT THE P'NIR HAD ASSEMBLED in the hangar, whatever it was, did not appear to be ready for use yet, and the guards with their hand weapons had retreated to the corridors, which were now closed off with some sort of shielding. The only P'nir in sight were a handful of workers attending to the final preparations on the projector, and those workers did not appear to be armed.

That being the case, Chakotay judged it safe to drop the shuttlecraft's shields momentarily, just long enough to use the transporter. At his signal Rollins dropped the shields, and Bereyt energized the transporter.

Kim and K't'rien flashed into existence in a

small auxiliary control room, one that K't'rien had pointed out on the sensor scans of the P'nir cruiser.

The room was not empty, but the sensors had warned them of that; Kim arrived with his weapon ready in his hand and promptly stunned the two P'nir working there.

He knew now where to aim the phaser, and to have it set on maximum stun; the exoskeletons still meant that the effect wasn't instantaneous, but the P'nir were too startled by the sudden appearance of their captain and a strange, ugly little alien to react properly—no alarms sounded, no warnings were given, and no weapons were drawn before the pair staggered, swayed, and went down.

"Now shut down the tractor beam," Kim ordered, pointing the phaser at K't'rien.

K't'rien moved to the control panels, and Kim realized with some amusement at his own expense that even if the P'nir captain had cooperated fully and told them exactly how to shut down the tractor beam, Chakotay or the others would have had a hard time doing anything with the information— the controls were designed for P'nir, which meant, at least in this case, that they were on overhead panels at least three meters above the deck. Even Rollins, the tallest of the four, couldn't have reached those without climbing up on something.

Kim told himself he should have thought of that; after all, he'd been the one who had roamed all those corridors where the inscriptions were all above his head.

Maybe if one person rode on another's shoulders, they'd be able to reach . . . but it didn't matter; K't'rien was here, and she would do the job.

"See this, small creature," K't'rien said, as she reached up with one of her four claws. "This is a control link for the main power system of the *Chugashk*—this ship we ride upon is the *Chugashk.*"

Kim nodded. "Get on with it," he said.

K't'rien ignored the interruption.

"Know that the *Chugashk* was my mother's before me," the P'nir said. "Know that it was built at the direction of my clan's grandmother, that we might be proudly represented in the vanguard of the great campaign to exterminate the Hachai once and for all."

"I'm sure you're very proud of it," Kim said, trying desperately to be polite despite the open boast of attempted genocide. This was not the time to make K't'rien angry; guards might be along at any moment.

"Yes," K't'rien said, as she simultaneously manipulated three grab-handles with three of her claws—again, a feat that a single humanoid would have had great difficulty in performing. "My clan has always taken pride in the *Chugashk,* and in our part in the extermination campaign." She swiveled the handles in an odd, intricate pattern.

Something about the way K't'rien was acting made Kim uneasy. "I'm sure you have," he said again.

K't'rien said, "The clan has never given up that

which is ours, little alien. We are a proud clan. We would prefer death to disgrace."

"I can understand that," Kim said, his discomfort growing.

K't'rien yanked at one handle, and a little panel sprang open. The P'nir reached inside for another of the odd little grab-handles.

"You see, alien," the P'nir said, "the *Chugashk* has secrets that are known only to my clan, and to my line within the clan—secrets that were built into it in case we might ever need to assert our primacy here. My clan, my line does not give up that which should be ours."

That made Kim even more uncomfortable. "The new captain, Tsh'pak," he asked, "is she in your line?"

He realized, after he had spoken, that he had not used the imperative, but apparently it didn't matter this time—either K't'rien was making allowances for Kim's alien speech, or she just wanted to talk.

"The line ends with me," K't'rien said. "I slew my sisters fairly, so that I was alone in the line, and ever since I have devoted myself to the war, to using the *Chugashk* well. I had never yet taken the time to choose an acceptable male and deposit my eggs." She made an odd noise, one that Kim thought might have been either regret or disgust; he wondered what would make a male "acceptable." Males didn't seem to play a very large role in P'nir society. Did K't'rien know that three of her captors were male?

"Tsh'pak is senior in the line of Ch'tikh, not in my line," K't'rien continued. "She is not even truly a part of my clan, but a part of a mere affiliate line, given honor aboard the *Chugashk* in recognition of the metallurgical skills of her grandmother."

That made Kim even more nervous. This all sounded ominous, as if K't'rien was explaining why she was about to do something drastic. She was still working at those complicated controls—why should it take so long to just turn off the tractors and open the hangar?

And why should she need to use that secret control, known only to her clan?

"Tell me what you're doing up there," Kim ordered.

The P'nir gave a handle one final twist, then looked down at the human.

"I have entered my personal code," K't'rien replied. "And using the secrets taught me by my mother and grandmother, I have commanded the *Chugashk* to destroy itself."

"You *what?*" Kim shouted. His fingers tightened on the phaser, but he didn't fire; if he fired, K't'rien would be unable to explain what she had done, and would be unable to undo it.

"If I am now unworthy to command the *Chugashk* in battle, then Tsh'pak is no worthier," K't'rien told him. "Better that the pride of my clan should be destroyed, taking you and your interfering companions with it, than that I should live on in disgrace, my authority never again certain."

"But . . . but you can be restored, I thought . . ." Kim stammered.

"Not while my captors live and go free," K't'rien said. "Either you four beings must surrender yourselves to me and go willingly to imprisonment, or we shall *all* die, and the *Chugashk* with us."

Kim tapped his combadge.

"How long do we have?" he demanded.

K't'rien simply stared down at him.

"Tell me how long we have!" Kim shouted.

"You must surrender within eighty-six seconds, or it will be too late," the P'nir replied calmly.

Just then Kim heard the rattling footsteps of more P'nir approaching—and approaching fast. Someone had apparently figured out that something was wrong here.

"Commander," he said, "K't'rien's set a self-destruct sequence here—she says she'll blow us *all* up if we don't surrender! She wants us as prisoners, and says that she can't be restored to the captaincy while . . . damn!" This last was as a pair of P'nir security guards burst into the room, weapons leveled.

They were aiming at P'nir height, however, so Kim was able to duck under the first shot and take one P'nir down with his phaser.

Aboard the shuttle, Chakotay and the others heard Kim demand to know how long they had; they heard K't'rien's reply, and then Kim's interrupted explanation.

"Can we get them both back aboard the shuttle

within that eighty-six seconds?" Chakotay demanded.

"Not and get the shields back up," Bereyt replied. "Sixty-two seconds now."

"Get Kim back here, then," Chakotay said. "Leave the captain where she is. She'll probably reverse the self-destruct if we do that—she'll be free again, and able to try to capture us. She won't blow herself up while she's still got a chance at redemption."

"Yes, sir."

Chakotay signaled Rollins, and the shields dropped; Bereyt began focusing in the transporter.

Then hesitated.

"Sir," she said.

In the auxiliary control room, when the first security guard went down, the second guard began spraying fire wildly. P'nir weapons were not true phasers; the handheld armament carried by P'nir security was little more than simple energy projectors, designed to blast whatever it was pointed at. There was no stun setting.

The guard's first wild shot took off her former captain's head; K't'rien's four arms flailed madly, and greenish-yellow ichor splashed in all directions.

The guard's second shot hit K't'rien in the thorax, and Kim heard the sharp crack as the former captain's exoskeleton broke open.

The head shot, Kim realized as he brought his own weapon to bear, might not even be fatal, since the P'nir's brains weren't in their heads, but it was surely crippling—K't'rien would have been blinded, at the very least.

The second shot had probably killed her, though.

And then with her third shot the guard had finally adjusted for Kim's height and crouched position and had swung her weapon down far enough; the beam flashed just as Kim fired again.

The phaser caught the guard in exactly the right spot, dropping her against the far wall, but it was too late—the P'nir beam cut deeply into Kim's side, and red blood sprayed across the captain's ichor.

Aboard the shuttle Chakotay looked at Kim's transporter fix and immediately saw what had happened, why Bereyt hadn't energized—the readings made it clear that K't'rien was already dead, and Kim might be dying.

And with them dead, could anyone stop the self-destruct sequence?

"Energize!" Chakotay barked. Then he turned and ordered Rollins, "The instant she's got him, get our shields up—maximum power! Throw everything we've got into them, and brace yourselves!" As the transporter hummed and Ensign Kim flashed into existence, Chakotay dove for the controls himself, hoping to warn the P'nir . . .

There wasn't time.

The shock wave of the cruiser's fiery self-destruction smashed against the shuttle and flung the four of them about like rag dolls. The energy flare overloaded the shields, and the feedback overloaded every system on board; the controls went dead, the lights flashed once and went dark. The hull rang like a gigantic gong, and everything inside shook. The rumble and roar deafened Chakotay and Kim and Rollins and Bereyt; for a long, long moment they existed in a dark emptiness flooded with sound, pressure, and vibration.

And then the sound faded, the pressure stopped, the vibrations died away. The silence was absolute; even the faint hiss of the shuttle's air system was gone.

Chakotay wondered for a moment, there in the dark, whether perhaps he had died and gone to join his ancestors in the spirit realm; then he wondered whether he was *about* to die, but not quite there yet, which would have been far worse.

And then the emergency lighting came on, and the backup power systems, and Chakotay knew he was still alive, and that he might yet manage to stay that way. He didn't feel anything broken anywhere, though he was sure he had collected a fine assortment of aches, bumps, and bruises during the initial impact.

"Hull integrity damaged," Rollins said, as the first automatic status readouts appeared on the one display screen that was operating. "We're losing air—several slow leaks, the systems are too damaged to pinpoint them, let alone patch them. Shields at three percent."

It occurred to Chakotay that yes, they were alive, but they might not be much longer. A slow death by asphyxiation would not be pleasant.

"Where are we?" he asked.

"Open space," Rollins replied. "Navigation is down, I can't get a fix on our location, and main sensors are down, but we're not under fire."

"What about the P'nir ship?"

"Gone, sir," Rollins said. "Totally destroyed. We're part of the debris cloud."

That might explain why no one was shooting at them, Chakotay thought; it might be that no one out there had yet noticed that the shuttlecraft wasn't just another chunk of wreckage.

That could wait for a moment. He turned to Bereyt. "How's Kim?" he asked.

The Bajoran knelt over Kim's battered, unconscious body, the shuttle's emergency medkit open at her side. "Bad," Bereyt said. "I've stopped the bleeding, but there's internal damage—he got thrown around when the explosion hit." She turned to Chakotay, a stricken look on her face. "I think he's dying."

"Is there any chance?" Chakotay asked.

"Maybe, if we could get him to some proper help," Bereyt said, "but I can't save him, not with just the medkit."

"Do what you can," Chakotay said, turning back to Rollins. "Do we have any propulsion?"

Rollins shook his head. "Not much," he said. "I wouldn't trust the warp core until it's been completely overhauled, after that impact. We've got partial impulse, but I'm not sure just how much, or how long it'll last."

"Commander, I don't think we want to move, anyway," Bereyt said, as she searched through the medkit for something else that might help. "It's a safe bet either the P'nir or the Hachai will shoot at us if we do."

Chakotay nodded. "Mr. Rollins," he said, "can you spot the *Voyager*?"

"No, sir," Rollins replied. "Not with the sensors in this condition."

Bereyt looked at Chakotay.

"What do we do, sir?"

Chakotay weighed the factors carefully. They were virtually defenseless, adrift in space a few kilometers away from the largest, fiercest battle ever recorded, a battle where neither side was friendly. One of them was mortally wounded.

Somewhere out there, though, was the *Voyager*. That was their only hope.

"We wait," Chakotay replied.

CHAPTER
27

"CAPTAIN, THE P'NIR SHIPS ARE CLOSING AGAIN," Paris reported.

"Then take us out, Mr. Paris," Janeway replied. "Outrun them, then bring us back in."

"Aye-aye," Paris responded. "Heading one-zero-nine mark two-two, warp three." They had discovered, in two previous exploratory passes, that even the P'nir's fastest ships could not hope to pursue them at anything over warp two.

"Mr. Evans," Janeway called, "is there any sign of the shuttlecraft?"

"Not that I can see, Captain," Evans replied.

Janeway frowned.

"Captain," Tuvok said, "I have just observed a curious phenomenon. A P'nir cruiser at the far end of the combat zone has just exploded—and has done so quite spectacularly, I might add."

Paris glanced up long enough to retort, "There's a *battle* going on out there, Tuvok—an exploding ship is hardly a big surprise."

Utterly unruffled, Tuvok replied, "I am aware of that, Mr. Paris. However, the circumstances of this particular detonation are rather peculiar. No Hachai vessels had fired upon it for several minutes."

"Old damage, Mr. Tuvok?" Janeway asked. "Emergency repairs that didn't hold?"

"Rather, it would appear to have been sabotage," the Vulcan said.

Janeway rose. "What sort of sabotage?" she asked, as she strode up the step to the security station.

"You think that our people might be responsible?" Paris asked.

"I do not have enough evidence to form a conclusion, Mr. Paris," Tuvok said, "but yes, I would certainly consider it a possibility that Commander Chakotay is somehow responsible for the ship's destruction."

"Let's go take a look," Janeway said, as she studied the sensor readings.

"Look at *what,* Captain?" Paris asked angrily, turning in his seat to glare at her. "If it *was* Commander Chakotay, then he's just blown himself up, hasn't he? We weren't there, ready to snatch him away with the transporter at the last second, this time."

"He might have found some other way out," Janeway said. "I want to see whatever's left of that ship, Paris, and I want us there five minutes ago."

"Yes, *ma'am,*" Paris said sarcastically. "I'd say that the shortest route would be right through the middle of the battle. . . ."

"Mr. Paris, I am in no mood for your attempts at humor," Janeway barked.

Chastened, Paris said nothing further, but laid in a course and engaged the warp drive.

Moments later, Evans reported, "The debris cloud from that particular explosion is badly scattered, Captain—much of it was caught in the perpetual cross fire, and it's gotten blended in with the general dust. However, there's a large chunk that looks as if it might be our shuttlecraft, or at least most of it. . . . It appears substantially intact, but I can't be sure. . . ."

"Get a tractor beam on it," Janeway ordered.

"Captain, it's too far away," Evans protested. "And it's falling further in toward the battle."

Janeway considered that.

"Are there life signs aboard it?"

"I don't . . ."

"Use the sensors, Mr. Evans," Janeway snapped. "That's what they're there for!"

"Yes, Captain," Evans said. A moment later he confirmed, "Four humanoid life-forms aboard—but one of them . . . well, life signs are very weak. Someone's badly injured, maybe dying."

Who? Janeway thought. Who was hurt?

What would the Maquis members of the crew say

if Chakotay died out there, on a botched attempt at a hopeless diplomatic mission? How could she carry on without a first officer?

What if poor young Harry Kim died? How could Janeway ever face his parents, when the *Voyager* someday found its way home?

Or Rollins, or Bereyt? The *Voyager* couldn't afford to lose *anyone.*

It looked as if they'd lost at least one, though, if they didn't do something fast.

"Mr. Tuvok, shields at full strength, please," Janeway ordered. "You're free to return fire if anyone shoots at us. Mr. Paris, you've been known to brag about what a hot pilot you are, and you've done all right so far—well, here's your chance to prove to us all just how good you *really* are. I want that shuttlecraft out of there and safely back aboard the *Voyager,* as fast as you can do it."

"I didn't prove it when I got us out of there the first time?" Paris muttered to himself, as he judged the situation. "I have to do it again?" Then he called, "Evans, you'd better have that tractor ready, because here we go!"

The *Voyager* shuddered, then charged forward, back toward the battle.

Aboard the shuttlecraft, Chakotay looked over the diagnostics and frowned. They had shut down every system they could spare, to conserve power, and it wasn't going to be enough. He let out his breath, and was dismayed to see a puff of vapor as he did.

"We're still losing air," he said. "If we don't find some way out of here soon . . ."

Just then the entire craft jerked violently, sending Bereyt and Chakotay staggering; Rollins, seated, was able to stay where he was, and the unconscious Kim barely moved. Rollins punched a button, turning the sensors back on.

"It's a tractor beam!" he called. "Got a good solid hold on us."

"A tractor beam? Whose?" Chakotay asked. "Hachai or P'nir?"

"Neither, sir," Rollins replied, grinning wildly. "It's the *Voyager!*"

For a moment Chakotay stared at him in disbelief; then he shouted, "Get those engines fired up, Rollins! We'll want to help them get us aboard!"

"Yes, *sir!*" Rollins replied.

CHAPTER
28

GETTING THE *VOYAGER* BACK INTO THE MELEE AND getting the tractor beam locked on to the shuttle-craft was the easy part, Janeway thought; it was getting everyone out in one piece that was going to be tricky.

The P'nir ships that had been harassing the *Voyager* before were still back at the far end of the battle zone, where the Hachai were keeping them busy. Thanks to the wonders of subspace communication, however, the entire P'nir fleet knew what was happening, and a dozen other P'nir ships came surging up out of the heart of the battle, charging toward the *Voyager* as it approached.

"Return fire as necessary, Mr. Tuvok," Janeway ordered grimly.

Even as she finished speaking, the foremost P'nir cruiser opened fire.

It was headed straight toward the *Voyager*, making no attempt to dodge or gain any positional advantage; Janeway could only guess that its captain was hoping to take them by surprise.

If so, the hope was vain. That direct course made it an easy target, and in short order Tuvok punched the phasers right through its shields and then through the full length of the ship itself, obliterating the P'nir ship's bridge and collapsing its entire forward structure.

Janeway didn't protest the inevitable loss of life; Tuvok had had no choice, with the ship coming straight at them.

The ruined cruiser sailed harmlessly past the *Voyager*, out into empty space, trailing wreckage and leaking a spreading cloud of atmosphere.

For a moment, Janeway wondered what would become of the surviving P'nir aboard the wreck; the phasers had destroyed the bridge and had surely killed the command crew, but the cruiser was large, much larger than the *Voyager*, and if the P'nir were halfway competent, they should be able to seal off the intact areas. Would another P'nir ship try to rescue them?

Then she saw a Hachai dreadnought pull out of the melee in pursuit of the P'nir ship.

There would be no rescue, nor would those P'nir have a chance to try to reach safety.

Neither side, she realized, was going to risk

letting the other attack its undefended worlds; no warship would ever be permitted to leave this battle in one piece, not even a broken one.

The P'nir ship's shields had collapsed when the *Voyager*'s phasers took out its central structure, and the Hachai dreadnought was able to blast the remains to powder in mere seconds.

In return, a swarm of P'nir ships converged on the dreadnought, and the battle once again shifted to include a new area.

The *Voyager* was back in the thick of the war—but the tractor beam was locked on to the shuttle.

"Captain," Tuvok called, "if either side realizes what we are attempting, the shuttlecraft will almost certainly become a target, and according to our sensors, the shuttle's shields are virtually inoperative."

"Then don't let them know," Janeway shouted.

"I do not see . . ."

Janeway didn't wait to find out what the Vulcan didn't see. "Mr. Paris," she called, "put us between the shuttle and the P'nir!"

"Aye-aye."

"Mr. Tuvok, blast any P'nir ship that goes anywhere near our shuttlecraft!"

"Understood, Captain."

A sudden crackle of static drew Janeway's attention.

"Chakotay to *Voyager*," a familiar voice said, faint and half-obscured by interference. "What can we do to help?"

Janeway's heart leapt. Chakotay was still alive and well!

That meant that it was one of the others who was hurt—Kim or Rollins or Bereyt—and she told herself she shouldn't take any pleasure in that, but knowing that her first officer was still functioning was a relief, whether she wanted it to be or not.

"Just hold on," she said. "We'll be picking you up in a moment."

"Captain," Tuvok said, "we cannot take the shuttlecraft aboard until we leave the combat area."

"I know," Janeway said. "We can't take it aboard while the aft shields are up."

"And lowering the shields while surrounded by hostile craft would be suicide," Tuvok said, completing her thought.

"So we'll just have to get to somewhere safe . . ." Janeway began.

"Captain," Paris called, "the P'nir are circling around, cutting off our retreat!"

"Keep us between the P'nir and the shuttle!" Janeway ordered, as she studied the viewscreen.

"But they'll block off . . ."

"Let 'em," Janeway said. She pointed. "Head for that sphere."

Paris looked up at the main viewer, and saw the mysterious spheroid directly ahead of them, adrift in the midst of the battle.

"But Captain," Paris protested, "we don't know what it is, or which side it's on!"

"We wanted to get a look at it," Janeway said, "and now we can. Do it."

"Captain, I must question the wisdom of your decision," Tuvok said. "I do not see what good it can do us at this time to approach the unidentified object."

"Tuvok, that thing isn't a new arrival," Janeway said. "It's been in there a long, long time, by the look of it—at the very least, it's been right in the thick of the battle since we first spotted it."

"I fail to see . . ."

"Don't you see?" Janeway said. "That means that Hachai and P'nir weapons can't hurt it! If they could, it would have been blown to dust by now. We can use it to guard our backs while we get the shuttle back on board."

"Understood, Captain," Tuvok said. "I withdraw my objections."

"Me, too," Paris said. "Working my way toward the sphere, Captain."

Janeway watched the battered shuttlecraft anxiously; the tractor beam had pulled it up close against the *Voyager*'s shields and was holding it there, off the starboard bow, while the *Voyager* herself twisted and dove through the blazing chaos of the battle.

Somehow, Tom Paris managed to keep that particular part of the ship always pointed at either empty space or a Hachai dreadnought.

At last, after five minutes that seemed like as many centuries, they neared the immense sphere.

"It's got some mighty big holes in it, Captain,"

Paris said doubtfully as they approached the derelict. "Are you *sure* their weapons can't hurt it?"

"It's still here, isn't it?" Janeway said. "Mr. Evans, what can you tell me about it?"

"It's an empty shell, Captain," Evans replied. "There are P'nir cruisers inside it."

"Maybe it's one of their orbital fortresses," Paris said. "If it is . . ."

Janeway shook her head. "No," she said, "Don't you recognize it? From Starfleet's first-contact records, in your history classes?"

"No, I . . ." Paris began.

"The First Federation," Tuvok said. "It had indeed been hypothesized, when no further contact was made after that initial encounter, that Balok's ship might have come from the Delta Quadrant."

"But it's just the ruined shell of one of their ships," Janeway said. "It doesn't prove anything about the First Federation; it could have fallen through a wormhole or just drifted here."

"I guess it proves that it wasn't built by the P'nir, anyway," Paris said.

Janeway nodded. "And that's all we need, Lieutenant," she said. "Take us in through one of those holes."

"Aye-aye."

A moment later the *Voyager,* after dodging one final P'nir barrage, maneuvered in through a jagged hundred-meter hole in the derelict's side.

The interior of the sphere was a maze of wreckage; chunks of metal glittered in the light of weapons fire and glowing, molten debris.

"Mr. Paris," Janeway ordered, "do what you can to keep that clutter from hitting the shuttle."

"Aye-aye, Captain."

"Mr. Evans," Janeway called, "open hailing frequencies—I want to talk to the P'nir."

"Hailing frequencies open," Evans replied.

Janeway stepped forward. "This is Captain Kathryn Janeway of the Federation starship *Voyager*," she announced. "We are claiming the interior of this object for a period of one hour, and we will destroy any ship, either Hachai or P'nir, that ventures inside it during that time. This will be your only warning."

She turned. "Mr. Tuvok, give them five minutes, and then carry out my warning—I want this sphere cleared."

"Captain, shields are at fifty-three percent," the Vulcan reported. "If the P'nir launch a sustained assault on us, they will be able to keep us trapped in here, and eventually destroy us."

"Well, then," Janeway said, "let's just hope they don't launch a sustained assault."

There were half a dozen P'nir ships inside the derelict, all of them relatively small; two of them fled immediately, but the other four fell into attack formation and swept toward the *Voyager*.

Tuvok proceeded to demolish the leader.

The other three broke off the attack and, after a brief hesitation, departed.

Janeway silently thanked whatever clever Starfleet designer had decided that it might be useful sometimes to use partial shields; the *Voyager* was backed up close to one of the hollow sphere's interior walls, with the forward defenses at full power, while the rear shields were down, allowing the shuttlecraft to be maneuvered into the shuttle-bay.

If the ship had still been out in the open, inside the ongoing sphere of battle, where enemy fire could come at them from any direction, lowering the aft shields like that would have been suicidal, but here, inside the First Federation derelict, the *Voyager* was relatively safe.

"Beam the wounded party to sickbay!" Janeway called, the moment the aft shields were down and the shuttle was clear of the lateral shields.

"Aye-aye," Evans replied.

Seconds later, Kes's voice said, "Harry's here, Captain. The doctor thinks he'll make it."

Janeway let out the breath she was holding.

"Good," she said. "Chakotay, get that thing aboard."

A moment later the shuttle bumped once, then settled smoothly to the floor of the shuttlebay—in one piece, and back aboard, with all three life-forms aboard still registering strongly.

Janeway, watching the pickup on video from the bridge, didn't wait for the big doors to finish closing; she turned to Paris and said, "They're aboard! Get those aft shields back up, Tuvok; Paris, get us out of here."

"Out of the sphere?"

"And out of the battle!" Janeway ordered. "Get us into clear space any way you can, and then get us away from here, warp eight!"

"With pleasure, Captain," Paris replied, as he reached for the controls. "With the greatest pleasure!"

CHAPTER
29

THE MOMENT THE *VOYAGER* BURST OUT OF THE SIDE OF the derelict four P'nir heavy cruisers began spraying heavy fire at it—not just energy weapons, but also high-velocity projectiles of some sort.

Tuvok immediately returned fire, but it quickly became evident that during the *Voyager*'s stay in the First Federation sphere the P'nir had analyzed their records, and had finally realized that it took *time* for the *Voyager*'s phasers to penetrate the P'nir shields. The cruisers were taking evasive action, dodging one behind the other, so that no single ship's shields were exposed for more than a few seconds.

That still gave Tuvok opportunities, but fewer of

them; he was no longer able to pick and choose his shots, or to target specific ships. Instead, to have any real effect, he had to fire at whichever vessel in the P'nir formations he could keep a lock on the longest.

Paris, who had had a brief rest during the shuttle docking, was at his best; the *Voyager* dodged, wove, and spun its way through the maelstrom, until some forty minutes after exiting the derelict it charged toward the outer edges of the battle—and was forced to turn aside.

A Hachai phalanx, a solid wall of warships each a dozen times the size of the *Voyager,* their shields interlocking into a single immense barrier, blocked their path.

Paris cursed, sent the ship into a roll, brought it around the edge of the phalanx, cut through a flock of P'nir ships, and headed for open space—only to be met, once again, by a Hachai barrier.

"What the hell is going on here?" Paris demanded.

"It would appear," Tuvok said, "that the Hachai are deliberately obstructing us."

"But why?" Janeway asked. "Mr. Evans, hail one of the Hachai ships."

Evans obliged.

"They're responding!" he said, startled.

"Onscreen," Janeway said.

The image of a multi-tiered Hachai bridge and its captain's transparent central globe appeared on the viewer.

"Greetings, honorable Kathryn Janeway," the

Hachai captain said, directing both its eyestalks toward her. "How may we help you?"

Janeway blinked in surprise. This was certainly a different reception from any treatment she'd received from the Hachai before!

"You can let us past," Janeway replied. "Let us out of here, and you can go on with your war!"

"Honored ally," the Hachai said, "we do not wish you to depart! Your weapons are splendidly effective against the P'nir; please, stay and wield them!"

Janeway suddenly understood.

"You don't still think it's P'nir trickery?" she said, bitterly.

"If this is P'nir trickery," the Hachai replied, "it is far too subtle for us, and we are fooled. You have wreaked havoc upon our foes; we humbly beg your forgiveness for our earlier doubts, and for all our misunderstandings."

"You're forgiven," Janeway said. "Now let us go!"

"But you will depart, and your weapons would be lost to us," the Hachai protested. "Stay and fight beside us! Is not our ancient enemy your own foe?"

"No," Janeway said. "We don't wish to harm the P'nir; we have merely defended ourselves. We came here to make peace, not war!"

"And what is a better peace than victory?" the Hachai asked, gesturing emphatically.

"A peace of cooperation," Janeway said. "A peace of mutual understanding!"

"Captain," Paris said, "if we don't get out of

here soon, the P'nir are going to be able to corner us against the Hachai screens."

"Hachai captain, whatever your name is, I ask you again," Janeway said, "let us pass!"

"We cannot," the Hachai replied. "Not when you offer us final victory, after all these centuries, after a hundred generations of Hachai have fought and died to destroy the P'nir. Would you taunt us so? Would you show us the prospect of triumph, and then snatch it away?"

"You're damn right I would," Janeway growled. "Listen to me, Captain—we are going to leave here. We can do it with your cooperation, or we can do it by going right through you. In case you've forgotten, our weapons can pierce *your* shields, as well as the P'nir's. Now, either you let us through, or we will *cut* our way through, and Hachai will die needlessly. It's your choice—what will it be?"

"Please, Kathryn Janeway," the Hachai captain pleaded, waving its eyestalks, "do not do this thing!"

"Then don't force me to it!" Janeway shouted. "Get out of my way!"

"Captain, the P'nir have us boxed in," Paris called. "I can't find an opening."

"Tuvok!" Janeway shouted, *"Make* us an opening! Mr. Paris, choose your course, and I don't care whether you take us out through P'nir or Hachai!"

"Aye-aye, Captain."

An instant later the *Voyager*'s phasers lashed out, and a second after that the red beams tore through the hull of a Hachai destroyer.

The Hachai ship shuddered and slid out of formation, leaving a gap.

Paris swung the ship about and slammed on the warp drive, sending the *Voyager* out through the hole where the destroyer had been—straight out into open space, at warp four and still accelerating.

CHAPTER
30

FOR THE MOMENT, ALL WAS WELL ABOARD THE FEDERA-
tion starship *Voyager.*

While there were still repairs being made, and
they were, as always, shorthanded, there were no
life-threatening emergencies. The engines were
working well, life support was functioning, the
hydroponics plant in the forward cargo bay was
flourishing; they were well clear of any inhabited
systems or hostile craft. All but one of the people
injured in the battle had been treated and sent back
to their duties; Ensign Kim had been the most
seriously injured, and was still under orders to rest
and take care of himself.

The Hachai and P'nir fleets were both far behind
them, with no chance of ever catching up.

The ship's department heads—and a few others—were gathered in the captain's ready room for a review of the ship's present situation.

"The *Voyager* herself isn't badly damaged at all," Torres reported. "The shields held up beautifully, all things considered. The shuttlecraft, though— well, we can fix it, but it's going to take a lot of work. It got pretty badly banged up when that P'nir ship exploded."

"Well, we have plenty of time before we reach home," Paris said.

The others pointedly ignored him.

"I did warn you, Captain," Neelix said. "I *told* you to stay clear of the Kuriyar Cluster. Didn't I tell you it was dangerous?"

"Yes, you did, Mr. Neelix," Janeway agreed. "Thank you for your warning."

Neelix smiled, then realized that the captain had definitely not said anything about heeding such warnings in the future; the smile vanished. He hesitated, then decided there was no way he could protest gracefully.

He debated for a moment whether to protest *anyway*—he didn't always insist on being graceful. Kes shot him a glance that decided him.

"Let it drop," her face said, and after another moment's hesitation Neelix let it drop.

"We still don't know where that tetryon beam came from, do we?" Harry Kim asked; he had insisted on attending, despite the doctor's orders.

"I believe we do," Janeway said. "It seems to have come from the First Federation vessel."

"From that derelict?" Paris said. "It couldn't have come from *that* burnt-out hulk!"

"The tetryon beam did, in fact, originate from the derelict," Tuvok said. "During our stay within the vessel I ran a full sensor analysis, and located a tetryonic device that had apparently still been functional."

"You put that in the past tense," Paris remarked.

Janeway nodded. "The device appears to have been energized by one of those energy weapons— probably P'nir. The beam struck it, activating and powering the tetryon generator for a fraction of a second."

"Captain, could we have salvaged the device somehow?" Chakotay asked. "Or could we reproduce it from the sensor records? Perhaps we could use a tetryon beam to contact the Caretaker's companion. . . ."

Janeway shook her head. "I'm afraid not," she said. "All that was left of it by the time we got there was slag—the same blast that activated it destroyed it."

"That," Tuvok said, "was why the tetryon beam's duration was so brief. The sensor logs will show you quite a bit about it, Commander, should you care to examine them—but not enough to allow us to build our own device."

"If you ask me, that derelict and its stupid tetryon beam weren't worth risking the ship over in the first place," Torres muttered.

"That wasn't the only thing we were risking the ship for," Chakotay reproved her. "We were hoping we could do some good, that we could give the Hachai and the P'nir a way out of their war."

"It's a shame we couldn't do more," Janeway said. Her voice turned bitter. "Instead of stopping the battle, we wound up fighting them ourselves— we did a lot of damage, probably killed hundreds on both sides, and for what? The war's still going on. I suppose it'll go on until one of them destroys the other, and even then, it'll probably just spread to somewhere else. Thirty years more in the Kuriyar Cluster, and who knows how long after that?"

"On the contrary, Captain," Tuvok said, "I am not certain that the war between the Hachai and the P'nir will continue more than another few hours."

Startled, everyone in the ready room turned to look at the Vulcan.

"Just what are you talking about, Mr. Tuvok?" Janeway demanded.

"As is standard practice in any such situation, I have continued to intercept both Hachai and P'nir subspace transmissions since we left the vicinity of the battle," the Vulcan calmly replied. "It would appear, from the communications we have recorded so far, that the two sides are negotiating, and that a quick cessation of their hostilities is a very real possibility."

"But . . . but . . ." Neelix said, "but *why?* The Hachai and the P'nir have been fighting each other for *centuries!* Their war is *legendary!*"

"Indeed," Tuvok agreed. "And all other sentients in this region have avoided them, as a result. We, however, did not. Our interference has reminded them that other starfaring species exist."

"But why should that make them stop fighting?" Janeway asked. "Why should they be suddenly interested in peace just because there are other people in the universe?"

"It would appear, Captain," Tuvok said, "that the Hachai and the P'nir are not so much interested in making peace with each other as they interested in forming a military alliance, joining forces against their common foe."

The others stared at him blankly.

"Against *us*," the Vulcan said. "It would seem that the effectiveness of our weapons, and the captain's ruthlessness in shooting at a Hachai ship that had just declared itself our ally in order to make good our escape, made quite an impression on both parties."

"Against *us?*" Paris protested. "But . . . but we're just one ship! All the rest of Starfleet's on the other side of the galaxy!"

"They don't know that," Janeway said, understanding. "We never told any of them where the Federation is. We never got that far."

"Exactly," Tuvok said. "It would seem extremely unlikely that the proposed Hachai/P'nir alliance will ever be able to locate its enemies."

Janeway considered that prospect for a long moment, then nodded.

"And by the time they do," she said, "they may well have forgotten why they were looking for us.

Peace might become a habit for them, just as their war had." She nodded.

"It's not the sort of peace I'd have preferred," she said, "but it's better than nothing." She looked at the others.

"Isn't it?" she asked.

About the Author

Nathan Archer was born and raised in New York City. As he was inspired by the movie *Metropolis,* Archer's great ambition as a child was to be a science fiction writer, but it wasn't until government budget cuts left him unemployed in 1992 that he seriously pursued the idea.

He got lucky.

His first novel was *Star Trek: Deep Space Nine: Valhalla,* which was closely followed by *Predator: Concrete Jungle. Star Trek: Voyager: Ragnarok* is his third, and he's working on an original novel as well as on other projects.

Archer lives in Chicago, has never married, and has no children or pets. His eyes are green, and other details are still classified.